HORSEBUGGY

Joshua Kornreich

Printed in the United States of America.
Set in Williams Caslon Text with LaTeX.

ISBN: 978-1-944697-74-7 (paperback)
ISBN: 978-1-944697-95-2 (ebook)
Library of Congress Control Number: 2018967344

Sagging Meniscus Press
www.saggingmeniscus.com

For those without grace,
for those who seek it,
and for those struggling under its weight

THE SWARM SWOOPS IN from every direction to pay heed to the Great White Giant. A giant city with a giant situation on its hands requires a mayor of giant stature—a gentle giant whose words reverberate more like whispered prophecy than bellowed admonition.

The horses, whispers the giant to the swarm. The horses must be spoken of.

The swarm watches and listens with hushed attention as the mayor moves his lips, spellbound as much by his pensive cadences as by his soothing utterances.

His decree: By executive order, it shall be, after ninety days, unlawful to operate a horse-drawn vehicle or offer transportation to the public on a vehicle drawn or pulled by horse. Any violator of said ordinance will be subject to criminal prosecution to the fullest extent of city law.

The swarm buzzes louder and louder before bursting into a rapturous drone. The savior of the city aims his enormous thumb upward and nods his massive head at the rejoiceful throng of believers, a head so white and so glowing, so hairless and so immaculate, that it transfixes the swarm like a sacred stone.

Another urban ailment remediated, the mayor waves farewell to his assembled audience, then exits the room, his squadron of dark-suited servicemen in tow, disappearing behind the very same curtain from which he had emerged.

The swarm disperses. There is news to spread. A sublime edict for the benefit of the community has been delivered. At last, the city is getting the moral direction it needs. This is a mayor the swarm can trust.

The swarm flies back to its orderly network of hives and disseminates the news pod over each and every news web: The Horses Have Been Saved, Long Live the Mayor.

IN A BARN far from the jurisdiction of any mayor of magnitude, a man with a crooked nose slumbers the slumber of drunken failure and dreams the dream of better days gone by. Days when the family farm was plush with greenery and cattle grazed the land as far as any young boy's eye could see. A time when chickens stood up on beds made of straw, and pigs rolled around in their mud pies, caked in their own slop. An age when men drove in from neighboring towns in rickety cars, their wives in the passenger seat, their little ones frolicking in the backseat, to pick up supplies, barter wares, make a sale. No difference which it was when it was all between friends. Everyone knew everyone on the farm. Everyone had a name, even the livestock.

One of the pigs had been given the name Junior, the same name imposed on the young boy that tended to it, though Junior was not the boy's real name, nor a name that the boy ever grew into liking.

How's Junior? the visiting tradesmen would ask, and the young boy's father, a disheveled man in gray overalls with scruff for a chin and grime for a face would say, Which Junior ya mean? The one out there in da mud or the one I'm gunna shoot between dem buggy eyes of his if he don't stop jumpin on the backsides of dem horses out back?

Behind closed eyelids, the man with the crooked nose listens to the words of his deceased father and gazes up at the night sky, aiming a pistol at the giant face peering down at him, its great white glow shimmering over the red and violet entrails of horses gone slaughtered. He cocks the pistol and waits for the right moment.

Mayor, the slumbering man whispers aloud into the pitch-black of the barn.

Mare.

Mayor.

Mare.

Mayor.

Mare.

Mayor.

Mare.

YA GOTTA UNDERSTAND—there were only sixty of us in the whole city, and he was one of them, ya see.

Short guy.

Funny-lookin too.

The kind of guy me and my buddies woulda beat the hell out of if this were high school or somethin, but I guess we were already past the age of doing that sorta thing. We used to laugh in trainin school behind his back when he wasn't in the room with us.

Ya see, the thing is, he was just so short, ya know? I mean, you've seen him in the pictures, right? Short all around with that long, crooked nose of his stickin out like so. I remember when they handed us out our driver hats after we got our licenses, and he tried putting his hat on, and I swear if the brim of it didn't cover him down to his eyeballs. He had to send it back and get a new one. Took him a whole month just to get a new one, and they don't allow you to start driving unless ya wear the one they give ya, so it ended up costing him an arm and a leg to just have to sit there at home and wait for one of them dumb hats to show up at his door. All cuz his head was too small, ya see?

Someone, I remember, some other driver said somethin about maybe he woulda been better off wearing it around his nose instead. Yep, all us folks laughed ourselves mighty silly at that one.

But, hey, you can say what ya want about him and his looks, but I'll tell ya one thing: he was a better driver than any one of us, yessir. I mean, the horses, they all seemed to like listen to him or somethin—I mean, like, really listen to what he was sayin and all. Like they already knew him or somethin. In fact, that's probably why he picked up on the whole thing faster than any one of us. Not that there was anything for him to pick up on, I suppose, now lookin back at it and given where he grew up and all.

But he didn't talk to any of us other drivers much. I don't think he ever talked to any of us other than to say hey or goodbye or somethin like that. He only talked to the horses really, or maybe the instructor on occasion whenever it was necessary to talk to him.

Shucks, I don't know. This might be hard to believe given now what we know about him, but I think a lot of us were just sort of envious of him.

Yessir, envy. Envy was what it was.

Sure, he was all funny-lookin, and he probably knew he was all funny-lookin himself, but it didn't seem to bother him none. And it certainly didn't seem to bother any of them horses none either. They just loved him. And he loved them back, for sure. Perhaps a little too much, I reckon.

But if what you're askin me is whether or not there was anything suspicious about him, the answer is no. No, not at all. Sure, he was real quiet and such, but last I checked, being quiet was not considered a criminal offense. Horse-drawn carriages, those are against the law now, but not being into talking—there's no law against that one just yet. Of course, if not being into talking was ever considered unlawful, that would fit me fine, cuz unlike him, I can go on talking all day. Just ask anyone who knows me and they'll tell ya I'm a talker's talker if there ever was one.

But I can't keep on talking with ya right here right now, no sir. I got me some customers coming in and need to set them tables up before I lose myself another job.

———⟨∘⟩———

SOMETHING TICKLES the sleeping man's face, and he awakens, his gray-blue eyes crusty and damp. It brushes him with strokes soft and silky, the fetid smell of barn manure wafting up his nostrils. He sees the stringy clump of his own fluid on the tail of his mare and the wooden step stool turned over on its side next to her.

My sweet, Gracie, the man says. Please forgive me again.

He gets on his hands and knees and searches the hay floor for his pants.

No pants.

He pats her backside. She is long overdue for a clipping, but that is the way he likes it on her—soft, thick and flowing.

Ya eat my pants, Gracie?

The mare offers no response, her competence with language hindered not only by the biological limitations of her species but also by her all-but-lost capacity for hearing words with her ears.

The sleeping man, now a woken man, picks himself back up and drags himself out of the stall of his beloved horse. A few straws of hay protrude from both sides of her mouth, her yellow teeth flashing in and out as she chews away.

The man grabs the straws from her mouth and lashes them atop her nose. Don't you go gettin too fat on me now, ya hear?

He ambles over to the empty stall next-door to have a peek.

No pants.

He drags himself over to the empty stall on the other side of his horse.

No pants.

The middle of his body aches. His stomach feels empty but his malnourishment is not what aches him.

He walks up and down the corridor, examining each empty stable for a sign of his pants. He remembers seeing them, on one occasion, somehow hanging from the rafters that hold up the roof of the barn, but this had happened just one time, and even as he now tilts his neck back to have a look, he knows it is in vain.

Something pricks his heel. A pebble in the haystack. He all of a sudden remembers he is barefoot as well.

So then, where are his boots?

In the farmhouse, of course. And if the boots are in the house, the pants are surely there, too.

They must be, he thinks.

Comfortable with his train of logic, the man with the crooked nose suspends the search for his pants. With his brain swimming in whiskey, it hurts too much for him to think about the whereabouts of his pants any further.

He stands half-upright and frozen in thought in the center of the barn, stark naked except for his flannel shirt, massaging his head back into what is, by his standards, more or less a state of conscious equilibrium. That bar for what he considers equilibrium has been lowered at an accelerated pace over the months since his true love passed away.

Grace.

Her name always on the tip of his tongue, no matter what his state of mind.

Grace.

He rubs his head with one hand and then rubs it harder with both until he realizes it is missing something.

His hat. Where's that gone now? In the house with the boots and pants? Hurts too much to think that one all the way through.

The sky is dark now outside the barn. Another day gone by without seeing the sun for this late-riser. The moon lurks around the corner. Time to hit the hay again. With a little shuteye now, his life might get itself back on schedule again by morning.

The man with the crooked nose stretches out his limbs and then looks back toward his mare, his other true love. He lumbers over to her stall and strokes her muzzle with the back of his hand and flicks the flies from her nostrils with his fingers, her mouth full of hay once again.

Gracie.

Grace.

Gracie.

Grace.

Their names—that of his mare and that of his beloved—swish back and forth in his head.

I'm givin you the night off tonight, Gracie.

The man with the crooked nose lays himself down behind the mare again, his small, cadaverous body stretched out across the hay floor, her tail swinging back and forth with hypnotic verve, bringing him back again to lighter times inside his dark and heavy head.

A SLENDER YOUNG WOMAN with a crooked chin looks on at her gentleman caller—a tall man with handsome yet prosaic features—as he attempts to hail down a cab in a city that stops for no one. The downpour from the sky shows no signs of letting up, and the wind and rain have twisted and pelted down their umbrellas into a contorted heap of cheap metal and drenched canvas.

We're not going to get one tonight, she says. Not on a night like this one.

Another minute, he shouts into the rain, his trench coat flapping in the wind. Another minute and we can go back inside and wait it out.

I don't want to, says the woman with the crooked chin.

What's that?

I said I don't want to wait another minute, and I don't want to go back inside.

What else can we do? The cabs are all taken.

They stare at each other in silence, waiting for the other to speak first.

I'm going back inside, says the gentleman caller.

Fine. Go back inside.

Are you coming with me?

She drops her umbrella into the trash can on the corner and turns away from the gentleman caller, leaving him to soak by himself on the deserted sidewalk.

The young man waves his hand at her. Let her soak, he thinks. Not his concern. Their plans for the night are already shot anyway. Besides, she could just take the subway home.

He watches her walk up the block through the window of the ground-floor convenience store until she disappears from view.

City girls. No patience.

She walks up a couple more blocks—the sidewalk more or less devoid of foot traffic—trots across the avenue between two slow-moving cars, and makes it to the opposite curb, but not before stepping into a puddle whose depth she underestimated.

The water from the puddle sloshes inside her shoe as she continues to walk. Fearing the shoe will slip off if nothing is done about it, she leans a hand on the wall of the base of a skyscraper and hops until the shoe comes off.

Her stocking is drenched to the ankle. A charley horse cramp creeps into her toes as she pours the water out and struggles to get the shoe back on her foot.

She eventually gets the shoe back on and continues to walk.

I will walk, she says to herself in her head.

I will walk until it stops raining.

I will stop the rain with my walking.

But the rain does not stop. Nor does the honking sounds of city traffic around her. A man rolls down his car window and whistles at her.

Hey, nice nipples, he says. Need a ride?

She does not look in the direction of the voice. She just keeps on walking. She walks faster and faster, taking advantage of the inclement weather to run the red lights.

The water feels refreshing on her face. She imagines the black eyeliner running down her cheeks, an urban ghoul in the night.

It is nice to be unseen.

A dozen or so blocks later, with no fellow pedestrians in sight, she comes across a city square—one that is, on most days and most nights, filled to the brim with human traffic, but not on this wet and windy night. She had walked through or around this very square many times throughout her life, but she had never stopped to sit on one of its benches.

Tonight that will change, says the voice in her head. It is her own voice, a raspy and defiant voice, but one that she has never amplified in public.

I will sit on this bench until the rain stops.

I will stop the rain with my sitting.

She closes her eyes, and lets the rain and wind caress her hair and face.

The sky begins to rumble, but she does not move. Every few minutes or so she hears a familiar clip-clop against the pavement in either direction, but she refuses to open her eyes to see its source.

I will not open my eyes until the rain stops.

I will stop the rain by not opening my eyes.

The wind gently unwinds itself, but the water comes down harder and harder. All sounds fade in the roar of the rainfall. As she stretches her petite figure across the bench, she feels herself drifting into unconsciousness. In her head, she looks down at herself from above, an angel on earth, drowned in her own tatters.

IT'S THOSE DAMN Chinese, at it again.

Christ, they're just buying up everything around here. To be fair, I heard they gave some Arab sheikh and some Russian contingent a tour there as well, but ya know how it is. Ya know it's going to be the Chinese again who get it. Well, I hope they pay through the fuckin nose if they get it. That's some prime property they're buying over there by the river. The city had been sittin on a gold mine—that's the real reason they ended the whole horse-and-buggy trade, if ya ask me. No moral reasonin behind it—just good, ole-fashioned greed.

Heard some people say they're gunna build some new luxury high-rises there once they get their hands on it. But then I heard some other folks say they're gunna turn it into some fancy hotel strip. I even heard one person say they're gunna build up a mall with a bunch of restaurants in it. I wouldn't mind seeing that, actually. If they do that, I won't have to drag my butt five miles every day just to go get me a burger and fries for lunch.

Better not be loaded with them noodle and sushi joints though. I mean, how anyone can eat that garbage, I'll never know.

But here's what's got me scratchin my head: what are they gunna do with them horses they got there? Last I heard, they still had them in the stables. I mean, are they going to buy them out too, them Chinese?

I hope not.

I mean, for the horses' sake, I hope not.

I hear they eat them over there, them Chinese—the horses, I mean.

Crazy sons of bitches eatin horses and buying up all our real estate—that's the Chinese for ya.

Ya think the mayor really cares so much about those horses if he's out there going to sell them out to the Chinese? Ya think he's really thinkin what's best for them horses or what will get him more votes? But it sure is convenient for him, ain't it? Get to have his cake and eat it too.

A mayor's mayor if there ever was one—that's our mayor for ya.

But he's a smart fella, that mayor is—I'll give him that. Not sure where his heart really is, but I'll give him that much.

Well, whether you heard it or not, that's my stomach calling. They only give ya so much time on the day shift, so I best get going. They always make ya feel rushed here in the cabbie business, and I sure do miss them buggies,

9

but I feel lucky I was able to land on my feet and get me some good benefits to go along with it, not the least of which is having a wife who wants to now stay married to me, if ya know what I mean.

I mean, I feel good again, ya know?

Just having a job again, I mean.

Not sure where my head would be if I didn't have this job.

In the oven, I reckon.

SHE FEELS HER SHOULDER being touched—that is what wakes her—but she keeps her eyes closed regardless.

Not until the rain stops, the sleepy voice inside her head whispers, as the morning drizzle pelts and tickles her cheek. Not until then will my eyes open.

Hey there, Miss, are ya okay?

Is that the handsome young man who was afraid of the water? She will never open her eyes then. Not for him.

Not for him? Miss? Miss. Hey, what do ya mean, Not for him? What do ya mean by that?

The man's voice is a beautiful baritone—not the higher-pitched one of her earlier suitor.

Miss? Are you having a bad dream, Miss? Are ya all right there?

The allure of his voice—she must see its owner.

She opens her eyes.

His nose. It is long, pointy and crooked. Morning scruff covers his chin and gray tartar coats his teeth. His top hat is beat-up and has a small rip at the top, exposing the stuffing. He looks like a man from another era.

This is not her handsome suitor—but that voice. . .

Miss? Are ya all right, Miss? You're drenched to the bone. You're shakin like mad. Don't look like ya belong on this bench here. I've seen a lot of people sleepin on this bench here over the years, but I've never seen the likes of you. Thought you was an angel or somethin.

She sits up and looks into the man's grayish blue eyes. They look older than the rest of him. She can see the traces of pain and loss inside them but also their warmth and sweetness.

Is there something I can do for ya, Miss? Are ya lost? Do ya need a ride home? I can give ya one. For free.

He nods over his shoulder. A horse-drawn carriage with a single brown horse. The horse has two purple feathers sticking up from the top of its head.

It's still raining, she says, wiping what remains of her mascara off her cheek. Can't believe it's still raining.

No, it ain't rainin, Miss. That's probably just the raindrops from the trees that you're feelin. No, it ain't gunna rain today. Sun should be coming out any minute now.

So that's yours? She points to the carriage.

Well, it ain't mine, really. It's my sponsor's. But that horse right there—she's been with me since the beginnin. We've been together so long, she might as well be mine.

What's her name?

Her name? It's Dulcinea.

Pretty name.

Yup. Whoever named her named her pretty well, I think. What's your name?

Grace.

Grace. Well, that's a beautiful name. Grace. Pleased to meet ya, Grace.

Pleased to meet you.

Their eyes meet in silence.

So, she says.

So, he says. Here let me help ya up.

Such a short man, she thinks. Without his boots, he is probably even shorter than I am.

Something wrong?

No, nothing. Just. . .cold.

Oh, right. Here, let me give ya my coat.

With one hand gently on her back, he leads her to the carriage.

I've lived in this city all my life. I've never ridden in one of these.

Well, I guess today's your lucky day then. Which direction are we headed?

That way.

That way?

Uh-huh.

With the driver's back facing her, the sound of the horse's clip-clopping feet against the pavement puts the young woman in a semi-trance almost instantly, but that does not stop the carriage driver from trying to make conversation.

Do ya like livin here in the city?

Sometimes.

Sometimes?

I like the anonymity of it.

Me, too.

You live in the city, too?

Nah. I'm from upstate.

Upstate?

Uh-huh. Take the train in every mornin.

Wow. Upstate. Must see a lot of horses up there.

Sure have. My family, we used to own a lot of horses.

Used to?

There was a fire.

A fire?

Yup. That's what I said. A fire.

That's very sad. To lose what you love. You probably loved those horses very much.

What makes ya say that?

I can tell. By the way you look and talk to this one. I can see it in your eyes, too.

Oh, so you can see it in my eyes now, can ya?

Well, not right at this very moment obviously—not with your back turned toward me—but I saw it when we were in the park by the bench. I could see the loss.

Really now?

Really.

He considers her words, then speaks again: So, tell me, Miss Grace, have you ever lost somethin you loved?

Yes. My mom and dad. The words slip out of her mouth, taking herself by surprise.

What do ya mean your mom and dad?

I mean, my mom and dad—they died.

Sorry to hear that. Mine did too.

They—they died together.

Oh, well, mine—they weren't together when they died. My mama went first, then my old man. I guess in a way they were never really together anyway. That's nice that yours died together though.

No. No, it wasn't nice at all. It wasn't nice. There was nothing nice about it.

Oh, I'm sorry. I didn't mean to—

It's fine. Really. It is. Happened a long time ago. It's the one over there by the way, she says.

She points to the rundown, brick walk-up between tenements.

Lovely.

Is it?

He winks and smiles at her. Here, let me help ya down.

Well, I really appreciate the ride. I can scratch another item off my bucket list.

It was my pleasure, Miss Grace.

She fumbles in her pocket for her keys.

Grace?

Yes?

If you ever need a ride again, just call this number.

He keeps his eyes fixed on her own and hands her his business card.

She looks at the card and looks up at the man settling back into the driver's seat of the carriage.

Is that your real name?

What's that?

The name on your card—is that really your first name?

Yes, it is. Why?

I don't know. Just never met anyone with that name before.

Me neither.

HE ALWAYS looked me in the eye. That's what I really loved about him versus the other boys I was ever with. He really seemed to listen, or listen right through ya, if ya know what I mean. And he was always on time. If he said he was gunna meet me somewhere at such and such a time he met me there on the minute.

He used to tell me I was beautiful even though I was fat. I knew I wasn't beautiful—not even close to beautiful. Plain and pudgy—that's what I was. That's what I've always been. And I think he saw that, too, but I still always believed he meant what he said. I knew what he was sayin to me really was that I was beautiful on the inside and that was good enough to make me happy. He just always knew what to say and boys are not always like that. In fact, I think he was the only boy I ever knew who was like that.

He did have a temper though—that's for sure. He would punch walls, kick the couch, curse, shout when somethin wasn't going his way. And sometimes he'd get really sad, too. That's when it was the hardest, cuz when he was sad he wouldn't talk and that made me feel kind of uncomfortable. Like that he might do somethin. To himself, I mean.

No, he never laid a finger on me. I mean, he may have grabbed me by my arm or my shoulders now and then, but that was just his way of gettin me to look at him—ya know, like really look at him when he was tryin to tell me somethin important. Like when he told me to never cheat on him, cuz there's nothin worse than being cheated on—that's what he said, I remember. He held me hard by both shoulders and that's what he said to me. But I can understand that. He was tellin me something that was very important to him, and I think sometimes his intensity got the better of him and he would grab me like that or point a finger into my chest. But he never hurt me none, if that's what ya wanna know.

And I never did cheat on him—at least not after he told me not to. There was this one time when we first started dating that I once kissed this other boy I knew since I was a baby, but it was more like kissin a cousin or somethin. It felt weird, and I didn't care for it much. But other than that, I never did anything with any other boys other than flirt some. But I never would've cheated on him, and I never wanted to.

He liked holdin hands—that was another thing I liked about him. Sometimes he wanted to hold hands with me when I didn't want to hold hands and that would make him kind of sad so I would end up holdin hands with him even when I didn't want to hold hands with him just so he wouldn't get sad and all.

It really made me feel sad to see him so sad sometimes. I guess I felt I had an obligation to make him not feel that way. At first, in a sorta weird way, I kinda liked it—being the one to make him feel better about stuff. But after a while, it became a bit of a burden, and I think that mighta been part of why we broke up. I mean, it wasn't just cuz of that that we broke up. There were other reasons, too. For one thing, he wanted to go all the way, and I didn't. I mean, we kind of did it sometimes—ya know, with our clothes on, I mean—but he didn't like gettin himself all messy from it, so after a while, he stopped doing that with me. And then before I even knew it, he wasn't even putting his tongue in my mouth or kissin my ear or even holdin my hand sometimes.

And then the thing with my cat happened. I asked him to take care of my cat one time when I went away on a trip with my ma and pa. He was really good at takin care of the animals on his family's farm. Even the horses, if ya could believe that. Did I tell ya he used to take me on his horse with him? I know. Kind of weird now, right? But I really liked riding with him. He would just have them horses walk real slow whenever we rode—no gallopin or trottin, I mean. I think a lot of the horses his family had were too old to gallop anyway.

But, yeah, the cat thing. I had him take care of my cat this one time, and when I came back he told me he had some bad news: the cat was gone. He said that he woke up two mornins later after I had left, and that he went to see where my cat was so he could feed it, and it was gone. Just poof. Disappeared. He said he was really sorry, and I could tell he meant it, cuz he had these real tears in his eyes and his voice was kind of crackin when he said so, but I was still mad at him for it. Not so much that he lost my cat, even though I loved my cat very much. But it's just then that I knew I could never marry him, and I could never have kids with him, cuz if he couldn't take care of a little cat, how could he take care of a little baby then, right?

Well, that's how I felt about it anyway. Maybe I was being too tough on him, I don't know. But that's why I ended it and that's why I told him I ended it. He didn't put up much of a fuss or even get that sad about it really. I think he had other problems—problems at home maybe?—that had nothin to do with me that were more on his mind than my cat.

We didn't talk for months after we broke up. I'd see him at school all the time, but we never talked to each other or even waved hello. But then one day—it was on a weekend, I think—he gave me a call and said he found my cat and that he was alive and well. Said he saw him down by the pond. He said he was hiding under a boulder and wouldn't come out, but maybe I could come with him this time and get him to come out. So, I walked up to near where his family's property was, right before the embankment that sloped toward the pond. He held my hand so I wouldn't fall. I didn't think much about holdin his hand or not holdin his hand when I was holdin his hand then and there, so maybe I still had some feelins for him at the time. Maybe not out of love but out of comfort, ya know?

Comfort was it was with him. I was never in love with him, I don't think. Think it just gave me comfort being around him.

So, anyways, he takes my hand, and we head slowly down the slope, and he shows me where my cat is, under this big rock, only I take one look at it, and I can see that it's not my cat. It's just lyin there on its back with its head bashed in—from the big rock, probably—and its eyes were all closed up and puffy-lookin.

It was dead, the cat.

I said to him that's not my cat, and he said I know it. So I says to him, Why are ya showin me this cat if it ain't mine? Why are ya showin me a cat that's dead and not mine, and he says, I just wanted to see ya again and just talk to ya again, that this dead cat under the rock made him think about me and him more than even my own cat being alive and well.

Or he said somethin crazy like that.

Me, I didn't know what to say to that. We just sort of stood there and looked at each other, me lookin at him, him lookin at me. Ya see, that's when I knew this was a boy whose mind was beyond my reach and beyond my help, and I just felt kind of bad for him, and I kind of felt not so comfortable being around him anymore, so I got myself back up the embankment and got the heck out of there.

Not that I thought he would ever hurt me though. He would have sooner hurt himself, I think, than hurt me, but I didn't want to stick around for that either, if ya know what I mean. I could only imagine what was going through that poor boy's head, never mind what he mighta ended up doing to himself.

But that's pretty much what I got when it comes to him. Thanks for listenin. It's a sad story, I know it. But then again most stories are sad if ya wait long enough for the endin. At least that's the way it works around these parts anyway.

Hey, listen. Speakin of sad endins, and not to rush ya outta here or nothin, but my husband will be coming home any minute now, and he hates when I tell that ole cat story, and he hates having people in the house when he gets home from work, and the last thing I need right now is him hollerin my ear off again. So, if ya don't mind, I need to go set up the table for supper.

You can just go on out the way ya came in.

THE MAN with the crooked nose and baritone voice takes the rush hour train home after his afternoon shift. He cannot get the elegant brunette he met earlier in the day out of his head.

Grace.

Amazing Grace.

How sweet the sound.

When he gets home to his empty farmhouse, he immediately runs up the stairs to his bedroom. He takes off his shoes, pulls down his pants, lies belly-down on his bed, holds one hand to his nose—he had convinced himself he could still smell her on his fingers—and shoves the other hand under his crotch. Rubbing himself through his boxers, he can still see her quivering, bubbly lips, her long neck, her dark wet hair, her see-through satin blouse, her moist miniskirt, and her exposed black bra strap all in his head. He imagines himself with her, soaked—from rain, from their own bodily fluids—and clutching her torso against his, locking himself into the holes of her being.

Grace.

Oh, Grace.

After he bursts through his boxers, into the center of his sheeted mattress, he lies there not moving, his eyes closed, fearing that the image of her would disappear forever if he did not hold on tight to it behind his eyelids.

Will she call me? How come I didn't ask for her number? What if she doesn't call me? What if I never see her again? Will I forget about her, the way she looked, the way she smelled, the rasp of her voice, on that bench and in the carriage? Was that rasp in her voice real or was she just under the weather from her night on the bench?

He at least knows where she lives—would it be weird for him to wait on her front stoop if she does not call?

Yup. Of course, it would be weird, he thinks. Very weird.

But, says the voice in his head: Her mama and her old man. His mama and his old man. Two lost souls meet in the night.

Or in the mornin time, anyway.

Inside his head, he sees her sleeping on the bench.

He rolls over and stares at the ceiling above him.

I'll never see her again.

His eyes follow the meandering brown cracks, the indents of the sheetrock.

One day this ceiling is gunna fall right on top of my head, but what do I care anyways? There's no one here waitin on me. Nothin but the grass and dirt outside.

Naked and sticky from the waist down, he walks down the stairs and onto the front porch. He looks up at the sky, but cannot see past the clouds.

Somewhere, on the other side of the pasture, deep in the woods, a bird caws.

THAT'S ME and him right there. I was Tonto and he was the Lone Ranger. I think it was the Halloween where they had a carnival for the whole county. They only did that one year, I think. At least I don't remember them doing it again. For all I know, they might have had it every year, but if they did, no one took me to it. Except that one. That was a fun one. I think that was an empty beebee gun he was carrying there. Me, all I had there was that plastic tomahawk ya see there in my hand there. Not so sure it was really supposed to be a tomahawk. Looks more like a hammer to me as I'm lookin at it now.

That's me and him again. We always liked racing on those. Bikes, that is. Mine was a Mongoose. His was—I don't know—a BMX maybe? Can't remember. But what I do remember is this one time when we raced down the main road—ya know, that road that has them shops on either side of it?— me on one side, him on the other, we raced each other to the train tracks, we did. Or, I mean, I did anyways. He kept on going. He crossed the train track, and just kept on going. Never lookin both ways, never lookin back—that was him. He just kept going and going until he was like a gray dot, that's how far he went. He never turned around and came back to where I was. He just kept going and going. Like a train, I suppose. I didn't see him again until a few days later, and when I did, he never said a word about it. It was like it never happened. But I guess you can say that's the way it always was when it came to him: like some things, or some stuff, never happened even when it actually did happen, if you know what I mean.

That one—okay, that one there—that's me, that's him, that's my cousin, and that's my cousin's girlfriend. Yep, that's him alright. He was starting to grow his hair long there. He wasn't into rock music or nothin, but I guess he just felt like growin it that way anyway. That's when his nose started gettin real long, too. Not big, I mean—it was never that big—but long. Much longer. And his voice was getting deeper, too, then. Of all my buddies, he hit his spurt before all of us even though he never really ended up growin much in the end. Yeah, that's me there on the left there. Never could keep my eyes open. I don't think it was cuz of the flash or nothin. Think it was just the way I smiled whenever someone told me to smile.

My cousin—he dated that one there from like middle school all the way up until he could drink and drive, I think. Or at least drive, anyways. See those on her teeth? Talk about train tracks, right? I never had any of those on my teeth, but I sure could have used them. We used to make fun of her for having them, and my cousin, he used to get real mad at us for it. But, ya know, now that I'm lookin at her again, I guess she was pretty cute. Not in that kind of way, but, ya know, like in a little daughter kind of way. Not that I would—oh, that one there? That's us at the roller rink—me and him, I mean. What did they call them pants? Parachute pants? Is that what they called them back then—parachute pants? Yep, that's me wearing them. Guess that was the hip thing to do back then. Not that I was ever hip or nothin. Nope. No one's ever accused me of that, no sir.

Let's see what else we got here. Oh. That's me and him at some random guy's birthday party. Friend of a friend of a friend. You can see there he liked to drink. And I'm not just talking beer. He liked the hard stuff, too. Probably got that from his old man—maybe his mama, too, I suppose. But he also liked soder. All kinds of soder. Anything that was black, purple, orange, yellow, green—he drank it, yessir.

Ah. That one. Ya see, that's his ole dog right there. He liked dogs. Liked them a lot. Not the way ya might be thinkin, but a lot. Looks like he's sleepin in that one. The dog, I mean.

Oh, would ya look at that? Kind of weird now, right? Seeing him on that horse? Kind of makes the whole thing hard to believe, if ya ask me. He was just so good to them from what I could ever tell. But ya know what they say about certain people behind closed doors. It's like Doctor Jekyll and—and—what's that one? I've never seen that one before. He musta taken that one while I was hittin the john or somethin. That's my mama, and that's our old livin room couch that she's sleepin on there. She was really proud of that couch, my mama was. Liked showin it off to people and tellin them how she found it.

Well, that's me and him there, too—I'm the one driving. He never liked driving much. Not cars, anyway.

And that one—that's the cat we found by the pond one time. It was all dead and lyin out there in the sun. We thought it was pretty cool carrying a dead cat around, if you can imagine that. We used to share it—some days he'd get it, sometimes I would. Stupid kid stuff.

That's him again. We were diggin a hole to put the cat in. Yep, that's him with the shovel there. And there's the cat again. It was starting to congeal really bad by then, as you can see, so he felt we had to bury it. I guess he felt it was the right thing to do at the time. I always thought we should have just tossed it back in the pond, but I guess that's just me.

Let's see here. What do we got? Oh, that's his dog again. Snoozin again.

Whoa. Where did this one come from? Is that a stick or somethin? What the—what was I doing in that one? Wait—was that me? Was that even me even? All you can see are the legs really, so it's hard to tell. Wait. Hold on a sec. Maybe that was—ah, ya know what? Come to think of it, that wasn't me. I just saw the parachute pants and thought that was me for a minute, but that wasn't me. No, that would never be me. That's them parachute pants I was talking about, but that wasn't me, no sir. Maybe he knew somebody else who liked wearing the same parachute pants I used to wear, but that's not me. No way I would ever be like that or do something like that. No, sir. Not me. Never. Never in a million.

WE GOT SOME good news for ya and some bad news. The bad news first: it's Dulcinea—she ain't pullin no more. Doctor's orders. Says if she keeps pullin the way she pullin, that bad leg of hers will split in two. I know how ya feel about her, so sorry to be the bearer of such news.

But here's some good news for ya too: ya gettin a new horse. A better horse, yessir. She young and she got herself some many years in front of her. And ya know what else: she's all yours. That's right. None of the others can have her on their shifts, ya hear? Just your shifts she'll be pullin. If I had it my way, I'd make it one horse for every shift for every man for everyone, but that seems to be only in your case.

And here's another thing that's only in your case: ya get to name her. Yup. Ya get to name her yourself. Turns out when they sent her with the medical forms and her number they forgot to put her name down. Or maybe they just didn't feel like putting her name down. Or, maybe yet, she was never ever even given a name even. Well, whatever it is, it's you who gets to name her now.

If I were you, I'd name her somethin simple. Somethin with one or two syllables maybe. But pretty. I always thought Dulcinea was a pretty name for a horse, but not so good for givin out commands—I mean, it takes too long to say it is what I'm sayin. Dulcinea. Too long. What's that—three, four syllables? By the time you get to the third one, she be trottin her heels on them cars, runnin red lights, tramplin some baby in its stroller to death. Maybe that never happened for you with her, but, well, then you were lucky, ya hear? Ya want somethin short and sweet. Short, sweet and simple, yessir.

Well, that's all I got for ya now. Keep your head up high and your eyes on the road. They're gunna take good care of Dulcinea, yessir. They ain't gunna give her the lights out like they do for some of the others. Nah, this ain't one of them cases. It's just that pullin them carriages—well, it's hard work. Backbreaking work. Leg-breaking, too.

But, no, sir—no need to shed a tear. She gunna be much happier where she gunna go, no offense to you, good sir. Yep. She'll be free to roam and eat all the grass she can eat. In three years time, she'll be so fat, you won't even recognize her.

So, here the keys, and just go on ahead there, good sir. That's right. Go on. Go meet your new lady. You'll be glad you did. She's three stalls down on the left there. Just be careful where ya steppin. The new guy—he missed one of them big piles of shit again, so you'd be smart to take notice, yessir.

And remember: two syllables. No more than two, ya hear?

THE BROWN-SKINNED orphan boy looks up and sees his own gaunt face staring back at him. His twinkling eyes follow the reflected images on the ceiling above: the lit candles, the silk tablecloth, the golden breadbasket, the glass bowl of caviar, the silver platter of roasted chicken.

And the wine glasses. He had never seen a real wine glass before. His is filled with water.

His gaze into the ceiling mirror comes to a halt when he recognizes the large, white skullcap of the giant man sitting across from him at the opposite end of the table. It looms over the table, glowing like a craterless moon in the dimness of the room.

The giant man points his wine glass up at the mirror. That mirror, he says. It's two centuries old.

The boy does not know how to respond. He is too afraid to respond. He fears his ignorance and inexperience will be revealed to the great and important man at the opposite end of the table. So he nods his little head and remains silent.

The giant man gulps down the red wine from his glass and places it down on the table. Where were ya born, son?

In the projects, sir. Somewhere in the heights, I think. At least that's where they found me.

Did they ever tell ya who your real parents are?

No, sir. They did not.

Is that somethin you'd wanna know?

Yes, sir. I would. I would wanna know.

Well, you shouldn't wanna know. You shouldn't be interested in people who aren't interested in you.

The boy clasps the glass of water in both hands. He still has not taken one sip.

But I can have it arranged.

The boy smiles uneasily. His grip on the glass is so tight now that his little hands shake, causing the water to sprinkle the napkin that covers his small lap.

The giant man winks at the boy and sips from his glass. His face turns abruptly sober.

This table, says the giant man. This table is too long for just the two of us. Why don't ya come over here and sit closer?

The boy slides down from his chair—it is too high off the ground for his feet to reach the floor—and begins to walk sheepishly toward the giant man. Remembering his glass, he turns back to the table to reach for it.

Don't bother with that, says the giant man. We'll just get ya another glass. Just come over here and sit here right next to me.

The giant man pushes out the chair next to him and pats the seat cushion.

The boy leaves the glass where it is and makes his way to the opposite end of the table.

Up, up, up ya go, says the giant man. He holds the chair steady and the boy hops up onto the seat. See, son? Isn't that better? Now we can see each other's faces up close.

The boy feels the upper half of his body stiffen as his legs dangle in the air under the table.

You are a beautiful child of God, says the giant man. His huge hand strokes the side of the boy's face, and the boy shifts ever so slightly in his chair.

I ask God every mornin to send me a beautiful boy and He sends me one. Amen, says the giant man, nudging his glass of red wine toward the boy. Please. Drink.

The boy stares at the glass in front of him. He has never had a sip of wine in his entire young life.

It's good for ya, son. I wouldn't give ya somethin ya wouldn't like. Go ahead and try and you'll see.

The boy looks up into the giant man's big, gray eyes. Only the deepest warmth and kindness are in them, his eyelashes like small, black feathers. The boy imagines how they would tickle against his soft, brown skin.

The giant man holds the glass as the small boy sips from it.

Amen, whispers the mayor into the boy's tiny ear.

Amen, says the boy in his own head. He takes another sip as a firm warmth comes over one of his thighs, and then another before lying back in his chair. He watches the glowing object in front of him edge closer and closer to his face until it swallows him whole.

MISS GRACE, your chariot awaits thee, says the horse-and-buggy driver with the crooked nose to the young woman with the crooked chin sitting behind him.

New horse, she says.

Why, aren't you the observant one this mornin. So, what do ya think of her?

She's beautiful. Very elegant. But where's Dulcinea?

They sent her away. Her legs—it was just a matter of weeks before they broke apart.

So, where did they send her?

Some farm somewhere. She'll be safe.

I'm sorry that happened.

It's okay. Besides, I like this one. She listens to everything I say. She's a docile one. I like that.

Docile, eh? You like your ladies docile?

No. I mean, sometimes. On certain occasions.

Excuse me?

Nah, I'm just kiddin ya now.

Uh-huh. I see. So what's her name?

Whose?

Your new horse, silly.

Oh. Right. Well, I haven't given her one yet.

So, she has no name?

Nope. Not yet anyways. I was thinkin it was like that song. He sings in his baritone voice: I've been through the desert on a horse with no name.

It felt good to be out of the rain.

So, ya know that song?

Yeah, I know it. Think everybody knows that one, no?

Maybe. Say, I think I know what to name her now.

Oh, really. What?

He stops the buggy and looks right into her green, almond-shaped eyes.

Gracie, he whispers. I'm naming her Gracie.

A BROWN BOY with thick, african hair listens for the footsteps of his stepfather coming from the hallway outside his closed bedroom door, but hears nothing, so he lights up another joint—one of several in his underwear drawer—and opens the window next to his bed to let the air in. Down below him, on the great front lawn and across the street from the mayor's mansion, he can see the men in dark suits scattered about at their nightly posts, ready to protect and serve the man who handpicked them for his security team.

But even with these men around, the boy never feels safe. Not with his stepfather always roaming about. What were all these night watchmen worth if the threat to his safety and the safety of his mother lurked inside the rooms and hallways of the mansion and not on the other side of its giant fences? And what good is a giant fence when the aggressor is a giant himself?

Sometimes he hears the footsteps in his dreams and sometimes he even hears them when his stepfather is not even home to make them. The sound— that heavy creaking of the floorboards—lingers in his head so much, that the only respite from it is the drag of a joint, the consumption of a pill—but even those moments of relief are short-lived for the boy. Who or what can cast aside the memory of a giant man creeping into the bed of his adopted son, numbing the child of its immediacy, its sensation, its damage? What buffer is there, real or artificially-induced, when the perpetrator lives with you day in and day out, eats at the same table as you eat at, and shares the same bed with the woman you call mother?

There is no buffer.

There is no relief.

There is no respite.

For this brown boy, the apple of his mother's eye, there is only the creaking sound of footsteps in the night, outside his very own door and inside his very own head.

YEAH, THAT'S THE GUY—crooked nose and all. What a fucking asshole he was.

So there I was just trying to pull into my usual parking spot in front of my office building, and that son of a bitch—him and his fucking horse—they were blocking me from getting in. So I started honking at the motherfucker and he was just sitting there with that stupid fucking hat on his head and those stupid fucking coattails of his ignoring my ass. So—what else could I do?—I set him straight, told him to move his fucking car, which he did, finally, and that was that. Or at least I thought that was that. Of course, I had to explain to the other partners at my firm why I was late to the meeting—told them about the guy and his stupid hat and his stupid horse, and for all I know they were probably all sitting there thinking I was making it all up. Probably came off like the-dog-ate-my-homework kind of excuse for people living in the nineteenth century.

Well, anyway, the day ended, and I left the office at my usual time, but when I got out to where my car was supposed to be it wasn't there. Instead, sitting there in my spot was that crazy son of a bitch on his stupid carriage with his stupid horse and that stupid fucking hat on his head. And I said, hey, motherfucker, where's my fucking car? And he was like, what? Do I know you? I think you got the wrong guy—and so on and so forth. I told him you know who I am and you know what goddamn car I'm talking about, and he said, oh yeah, I remember you now—you're the busy man, and at first I was like what the fuck do you mean the busy man, and then I realized he was talking about my license plate—it says BIZ ZMAN on it, with two zees—some silly joke my wife came up with when she bought the car for my birthday. So, now I'm like, okay, where's my fucking car since you apparently remember what my license plate says, and he goes I think I saw it around the corner over there, and I'm thinking this guy, he's a really crazy son of a bitch, but, you know, for whatever reason I followed his direction, and, lo and behold, it was there, just around the corner, unharmed—or so I thought, anyway. One of the front wheels had been pulled onto the curb. I was thinking whoever did this—whether it was this crazy son of a bitch or someone else he put up to this—whoever it was must be one lousy fucking driver to park a car that way.

So anyway, when I opened the car door, I got this big whiff of something nasty, but I didn't know what it was at first. So, I get in and I open my glove compartment for my sunglasses—they're my prescription ones for driving—and I reach in there with my hand, but when I pull it out, there's this big ball of turd—I mean like human turd—just sitting inside there. I think I fucking screamed. But then I was like fucking pissed—I mean, I'm fucking fuming, right? I mean, I just wanted to go back and beat the crap out of that little son of a bitch—but as soon as I turn around, there he is, sitting up on his carriage, with his fucking horse right in front of him and that whip of his that those buggy drivers use to lash their horses with to make them go. And he's just staring at me—he's not smiling or anything. Just staring. Very sober stare. I have to admit—the way he just stared at me with that whip in his hand—it scared me quite a lot. I think I said to him, well, what did you do that for, and he said I didn't do nothin, I barely even know how to drive a car, let alone parallel park. He said it was probably one of them homeless people going for a joyride, trying to steal what he could steal and then left a present for me.

Left a present—I remember him saying it like it was some kind of joke to him, only, like I said, he wasn't smiling at all.

I probably should've called the cops right then and there, but I didn't, and not because I was afraid with him right there—I mean, I was afraid with him right there, but that wasn't the reason. No, what it was was that I actually convinced myself that he was telling the truth—that it was probably some homeless person who played some kind of sick joke. I mean, there's a lot of stuff going on these days—that sort of class warfare stuff, I mean. I was thinking whoever it was just wanted to take out his anger and frustration on my car because I'm rich and he isn't. So I said to myself, oh fuck it, and just live and let live. So I just went ahead and rolled the windows down, and pulled out of the parking spot. That son of a bitch driving the carriage, he just tipped his hat at me and told me to drive safely.

I drove the car straight to the service station—figured I'd have them clean it up good. Had my wife come and pick me up there with her own car—told her all about it. She couldn't believe it. Then, when we were just about to pull into our driveway, my phone rings, and it's one of the guys from the service station. Told me to come right back and come take a look at this. So, we get ourselves back to the station and there's the service guy, holding a rag over his nose and mouth, with the trunk of my car wide open. He said to come over and take a look, so I did. If I told you it wasn't packed to the brim with the biggest steaming pile of horseshit anyone's ever seen, I'd be lying to you. It reeked so fierce that my wife took one look at it and hurled all over the blacktop.

I called up the cops, of course. Filed a report. Told them everything that happened and about that motherfucker and his fucking horse carriage. They took a preliminary inspection of my car and said it didn't turn up any fingerprints or footprints, and having no witnesses presented a problem. They probably thought it wasn't worth their resources investigating any further, but whatever—I already knew who did it. They said to call them right away if I ever saw the guy again. But I never saw him. It was like a ghost took a dump and then just left. Two ghosts, if you include that fucking horse of his.

Now, when I go to work, I just park my car in the garage—they charge you through the nose, but at least I can afford it, and at least I don't have to worry about running into that crazy son of a bitch no more. I mean, for weeks after the incident, I kept looking over my shoulder. And not just here in the city—I mean, who knows what kind of information he had on me. On my wife. On my children. I mean, he was sitting in my fucking car, for christ sake.

Eventually, though, I stopped thinking of him. Chalked it up as just being one of those weird stories that happens sometimes in a man's life. I think I had put it out of my mind for months until I saw the mayor make that speech— you know, that one where he banned them horse carriages? Man, that put a big fucking smile on my face when that went down. But given the way that crazy motherfucker acted with me, I could see how that probably set him off—that, and probably whatever it was that had set him off in life to begin with.

It's envy—that's what it is, plain and simple. Man sees something he doesn't have and never will have, and that leads to envy, which leads to anger, which leads to violence, which leads to someone getting killed. No one wants to be reminded about what they don't have. Perhaps in rough times like these, those of us who have a little more than others—well, maybe we should tone it down a bit. I mean, at least that's what I did anyway: I ended up selling the car a few months back and got myself a new one. Less expensive, but runs a whole lot better. Safer too. I even changed the message on the license plate to a bunch of random letters and numbers.

But don't let that fool you now: I'm still one busy son of a bitch.

YOU LIVE HERE? You grew up here? Whoa. I mean, it's—it's beautiful. Just beautiful. Those trees. I don't think I've seen such beautiful trees in all my life. It must be so nice to wake up to all of this every morning, being so close to nature and all. Is it? Must be. I always wondered what it would be like to live on a farm or a ranch. Tending to crops, to livestock. I mean, not that you have any of that here now, but you once did you said, right? Must've been such an experience for you, having all that, right? Or is it so long ago now, that you don't remember it all?

So lovely here. The air. Just lovely. And calm. So calm. Birds—the sounds they make—it makes me feel calm. You know, like inside? About life? And the trees too—they're so, like, soothing, you know?

Yep. I can get used to this.

So, is that the barn over there? Can we go in there? I know you said there isn't anything in there anymore, but I'd love to see it anyway. There's something about barns—maybe it's their architecture maybe?—that just makes me feel in awe and at peace at the same time. Or maybe it's just the smell of barns that gives me that sort of feeling—I don't know.

Do you ever stop and think about that kind of stuff? About smells and everything? Or are you just so used to living here all your life that you don't even think about it? You don't, right? I figured. You must feel the same way about cities that I do about farms, the country—only the opposite though, right? I hate the air in the city. I mean, I'm used to it, but I hate it, you know?

But I guess you kind of like the city, right? I mean, you could've gotten yourself a job up here instead—maybe not as a farmer or a rancher or something, but maybe doing something else closer to home. So, I'm guessing that means you like the city, right?

By the way: I think it's so cool that you don't own a car. It's like you're the real deal, you know? I don't know, it's tough to explain. Or maybe I'm just not making any sense here at all.

But I have to say, that house—as much as I like the whole wrap-around porch thing—it could use some work. No offense. I mean, maybe I'll change my mind a bit once I go inside it, and I'm sure it's got some great bones to it, but from the outside—I mean, when's the last time you painted it? I mean, you got to paint that, no? Maybe if you invite me over here again, we'll paint it together. Deal? Deal.

All this open space. Must give you a lot of room to think. Ever get lonely here? Don't answer. Stupid question. It's not like because there are so many people in the city and so many buildings and things that you can't get lonely there, too. I mean, I've felt lonely and I've lived in the city all my life. I think being lonely has less to do with where you live and what's around you and more to do with what's in here—your head. And here—your heart. I mean, maybe your environment—your physical environment, I mean—can push it one way or the other way, but I think it's more about what's going on inside more than the outside—know what I'm saying? Do you?

You know, you're really quiet. I think you're the quietest person I ever met. I mean, I'm quiet too usually, but I think because you're so quiet, that I'm less quiet when I'm around you—sort of like filling in the empty space. I mean, I don't mind that—it's easy talking to you. I can tell you're a good listener. And there's something about you that makes it easy to talk to you, which I like, because I've probably kept a lot of things pent-up when I've been around other people. And when you do talk and all, it's really interesting, what you have to say. But it's almost like—well, you know how's there's a lot of open space here? And you know how like you said it used to be not all open space, but there was all this livestock, like horses and cows and goats and stuff and now you can't see them because they're not here anymore? Well, that's how it sometimes feels when I'm around you. Like you have this open space around your head or something or in your heart or something that was once filled with joy or passion or desire or love or innocence or whatever, and now it's like disappeared, or been stripped even, over time—from your experiences, I mean. Or maybe certain experiences that you had maybe? I mean, you're not easy to read is what I'm trying to say. Like this whole place isn't easy to read—it's like you look at it and, yeah, it's nice, gorgeous even, but at the same time you're like what happened to it? How did it end up this way? It's like how did you end up whatever way you ended up is I guess what I'm saying here, you know?

But maybe what I'm saying here is really about myself here and not you. I mean, I barely know you, right? So far, anyway. It's just that there's so much open space, so much open air—how do you fill it in, you know? And maybe that's why you haven't tried filling it in—all this space—because there's just too much of it to fill in out here, and in your head, and in your heart.

Am I making any sense here? It's okay if I'm not. It's just that it's so open, wide open, out here that—well, it makes me want to be open with someone. With you, I mean. And I—I just want you to be open with me too because so far you haven't been.

There, I said it.

How MUCH you want for her? says the man with the crooked nose.

How much you willin to pay? says the old stableman.

Nah, I'm not playin that game. You tell me what your ask is. And then I'll tell ya what I'm willin.

What do you want her so bad for?

She's my horse. I know what you folks are going to do to her if no one buys her.

We ain't gunna be doing nothin to her. It's the city. It's the mayor's office. They're the ones who put the ban on us. It's up to them now what they want to do with her—not us. I'm not really allowed to be doing this—you know that, don't ya?

Yessir.

So, what are ya gunna pay me for my troubles then?

How about two hundred?

Two hundred? You think two hundred is going to reward me for the risk I'm taking with this?

She's a depreciated asset. Ya said so yourself. I'm willing to pay two for a depreciated asset. I think that's fair.

Depreciated or not depreciated, don't make no difference to what's at stake for me. If anyone so far as has a sneakin suspicion of what I'm up to, I'll get canned. Canned and blacklisted.

Fine then. What's your ask?

Six.

Six hundred?

Yup.

Six hundred for a depreciated asset?

Yup. Six.

Well, I ain't payin that.

Well, I can understand that. Six for a depreciated asset is probably asking a lot of ya. But, like I said, there's risk for me, too, here. I need to be able to take some consolation for some unforeseen damages to my professional— what's the word?—reputation.

I hear ya loud and clear. But I can't pay that much. Needs to be lower.

Nope. Can't be lower. Hey, look at this way: One, she's not exactly young anyway, so who cares if the city gunna give her the lights out. And, two, if another buyer comes—

Another buyer? What other buyer?

Well, ya think you're the only one askin me what the ask is on these horses?

Who is it that's askin about buying? One of them other drivers?

Them drivers, some rich people, some ranchers and farmers from all over—that's who. I even got a chinaman askin me, but I ain't sellin to him, no sir. Horse is like a delicacy over there, I think. Or maybe it's just dogs. Anyway, I don't want any of our own endin up in someone's chopped suey, if ya know what I mean—wouldn't feel right, no matter the price.

Look, you know I'd pay six if I could, but—

Five. I'll take five. It's five, take it or leave it.

You son bitch.

Yeah, yeah—take a walk then if you ain't takin her.

Four, then.

What's that?

I said four. That's twice more than my original bid.

Twice more, eh? Tell you what: let's make it twice-and-a-quarter more.

What do ya mean, twice-and-a-quarter more?

What do ya mean what do I mean? What I mean is twice-and-a-quarter your original bid. What I mean is four-fifty all-in, including transportation.

Four-fifty all-in?

Four-fifty all-in. Man, if you're not willin to take your own horse for four-fifty all-in—this horse who's given her entire body over, never mind her mental health, in order for you to have earned yourself a decent livin—then you ain't fuckin deservin of her then.

Four-fifty all-in, huh? Shit, man. Fine then. Four-fifty it is.

Sold. Since I like ya, I won't charge ya for any city sales tax.

Son bitch.

Right back at ya.

A MAN WITH a crooked nose and a younger woman with a crooked chin lie on their backs, next to one another, on a blanket laid across the dead grass at the foot of a gravel driveway that separates them from the front porch of an old and broken-down farmhouse.

It is a full moon, less the occasional passing cloud. Stars are everywhere, but neither knows how to read them.

They died many years apart, he says. She was kind of young when she died. Not much older than I am now. Said it was the fever, but if it was the fever, then it was her love of drink for so many years that had made it worse. Her body was just not in any condition to fight off anything, never mind the fever. But I hardly knew her, really. She never said much. I don't think she had the strength to say much on most days. She never looked at me. She was always lookin for something else. Her flask. A bottle. But never me.

My old man, he was different. He paid a lot of attention to me— sometimes too much attention. His attitude was more like never mind your mother. Never mind your mother, boy—just go on and do what I told ya. That was him, alright. He drank as much as her, but his head always seemed clear most of the time. Clear enough to tell me what to do and whip me some whenever I didn't do it, anyways. But his body, all his organs—they all went to shit. Had himself cremated. Drinkin, smokin—he did a lot of both all the time. Made the whole house stink. It still stinks from him in there. He wasn't too fond of cleanin himself. Figured it was dirty work livin on the farm—just gunna get all dirty again anyways, so what's the point? But that was him, too—it was all about having a point. I don't think I ever found my point. In that way we were different, but I'm not stupid enough to not believe that in some ways I'm like him. Love of drink—that's me for ya, too. And some other stuff.

He takes another puff of the joint between his fingers before passing it to the young woman.

The young woman takes a drag of her own and blows out. She's never seen so many stars in her life.

Mine, she says—they died together on the same day. Maybe even the same time—or at least that's how I'm used to imagining it. I remember very few things before it. I was just a little girl. They were never happy—at least not around me, anyway. I've gone through their old photo albums—their wedding day, their days together before they got married, and some from when they were kids, too. They looked happy. Really, truly happy. There are some photos of me, too, in them—back when I was an infant. They look happy in the earlier ones, when I was first born. Then with the later ones it's like they look tired, sad—empty. Like they realized they lost something. I mean, I don't think it was just me that made them that way. I think—I don't know. I think they just realized they were too young to be so committed to something—that's how I see it, anyway. I think they loved me, but sometimes wished they hadn't had me. Nothing personal against me—no, I don't think that, no. Just that—well, it was like I was in the way of what they wanted and it depressed them even more knowing that I, the one they were supposed to love more than anything in this world, was in the way of all that. I think they had a lot of love for each other and they didn't want to share it with anyone else—not even their own little daughter. And even though I was just a little girl, I think I understood that about them even back then—that I wasn't as important to them as they were to each other. I remember days when my carpool for school would drop me off at home and they wouldn't be there. They would just leave the key in an envelope that they would wedge into our apartment door. No message. No I'll-be-home-soon. No dear, no sweetheart, no honey, no love. Just a key inside an envelope. They would get home late—sometimes together, sometimes not together. When they came home together, I would sometimes hear them giggling with one another coming out of the elevator, and then the laughter—it would all of a sudden go away when the door creaked open and they tossed their keys on the counter. That went on for—I don't know, to me at the time, it seemed like years. Then all of a sudden that stopped. They started being there, together, in the living room, in front of the TV, whenever I got home. They'd see me, force a sort of glazed smile, ask me how school went. It was like they wanted to care, but they couldn't. Sometimes it felt like I interrupted something between them whenever I came home or entered the room. But I still liked seeing them there on that couch—it allowed me to think things were normal among us. But it never was. They stopped smiling. They stopped saying anything to me when I got home. I read my books in bed by myself. I put myself to sleep. I invented the words to lullaby melodies that I might've once heard. Then one day, I came home from school, and there they were again, on the couch, their hands touching, their eyes closed. There was an almost-empty glass on the coffee table in front of them. I took the glass, poured the rest of the water that was in it into the sink, and then tiptoed into my bedroom, so I wouldn't wake them up—I always wanted to be a good daughter to them, no matter how they felt about me. I did my homework in my room. I had a bowl of cereal for dinner—the same as the other nights they forgot to feed me, or didn't bother to. But I was happy, or forced myself to be happy, because at least they were home. The next morning, they were still on the couch, sleeping. I figured they must've been up at some point, but then went back to sleep on the couch—wouldn't be the first time they ever did that. I could see that my dad's head was a bit slumped over and leaning to the side. His tee-shirt looked wet at the chest—like he had drooled on himself or something. I remember trying hard not to giggle. It wasn't until I left the apartment and got in the elevator that I let myself laugh out loud. I even remember telling someone in my carpool on the way to school about it.

When I got home, my dad's head was on the couch. It looked kind of awkward, the way it was twisted in its position. My mom was still in the same position. She looked pale. I said, Mom. No answer. Mom, Dad. No answer. I was just a little girl. I thought they were in another one of their deep sleeps. I barely slept that night. I woke up in the middle of the night to pour myself a glass of water from the sink. When I went back to the living room, instead of going back to my room, I sat there and watched them sleep. My dad's body slipped onto the floor. I can still remember the thud his head made when it bumped into the coffee table. My dad stayed asleep. So did my mom. She never budged at all those two days. Just her skin changed.

I was so busy watching them, imagining that they were alive, pretending I didn't know what death was, that my friend's mom had to buzz up to let me know everyone in my carpool was waiting outside. I told her I was still in my pajamas and that my parents had been sleeping on the couch for two days. She came up and saw them and said nothing. Took me and the others to school, dropped me off in a room next to the principal's office. I stayed at a friend's house that night. It wasn't for another two days later that I think it finally sunk in.

The woman with the crooked chin takes another drag from the joint and hands it back to the man with the crooked nose.

Cyanide, the young woman says. That was the postmortem.

Fuckin shit, the young man says. That's about the worst—excuse me, I'm sorry.

It's okay. That's pretty much everyone's reaction when I tell them—not that I've told many people.

Yeah, but it's no excuse. I'm sorry for sayin that.

It's okay. She turns and lays the back of her hand against his cheek. So, how about you?

How about me what?

Think you'll ever find your point?

38

He takes another puff from the joint. Nah. I mean, I don't know. I mean, I guess when I'm with you, I—

The man with the crooked nose cannot continue as his eyes find hers staring right through his.

Hey, it's okay, says the woman with the crooked chin. You have time. We have time. She rolls on top of him, mounts him through her jeans. She grabs the joint from his fingers and flicks it away.

His body feels limp all over.

I can't, he says. I mean, I wanna, but I just can't. Not right n—

I know. It's okay. There will be other times. Lots of times.

She lowers his head onto his chest.

Your heart, she says. It beats so fast.

He strokes her hair with his hand. It feels like the mane of the most beautiful mare he has ever touched.

YEP, THE TWO of them—they were very much in love, yessir. They clung to each other a lot. Used to see them on the main street on the weekends, walking in and out of the shops. Came into my parlor lots of times. For as long as I can remember, ever since he was a boy, he always liked chocolate. Never liked vanilla. Never ordered it. Never called it chocolate neither. Rocky road is what he called it. I remember when he and his old man used to come in here. Rocky road, Pa, is what he would always say to his old man, and then his old man would say one vanilla for the boy, and then the boy, he would get all worked up, but of course he always got his rocky road.

But she—well, she sure was a beauty. Well, for a gal with a crooked chin anyways. But she would come in, and she would always order for the both of them. Chocolate chip, mint chocolate chip, coffee chip—anything with chip in it, she would order it, and they would both eat it. Sometimes she would just order one cone for the both of them. They'd be takin turns lickin that same mint-chocolate chip cone, not thinkin once about givin each other germs or nothin. She eyeing him. He eyeing her. You could just tell they just had it on for one another.

Sometimes I wonder how much she knew about him. I mean, not that anybody really knew him well around here, but we all heard stories. About him and his mama. Him and his old man. Him and them animals they had.

Ya know about their barn, right? About the fire? Ya know, some say it was him that did it. Hell, I didn't know what to believe, but that's what some people said. That he was a bad kid. That he wasn't born right. That he wasn't raised right. That he wasn't raised at all.

But me, I always kind of thought he was a good kid—as far as I could see, anyway. To me, he was just that little kid who came in with his old man, wanting that rocky road. Nothin seemed that off to me about him. A bit dirty-lookin maybe, but given where he was livin and the way he was livin it made sense that he was.

Now, she—she was from the city now, right? She had that big-city-look to her, but sorta—what they call it?—bohemian-lookin? Yep, that was her alright. Refined, sure, but somethin dirty lurkin underneath that urban exterior. Could see it in the way she was lickin that ice cream cone. Always looked like she was lickin somethin else, if ya know what I mean. But nice girl. Yep. Nice girl. Some rumors about her shopliftin some of them stores out on the main street when she first started coming out here, but I never paid them any attention. Besides, who steals ice cream anyway? But I tell ya, it's a goddamn shame what happened to her. Too young. Way too young for somethin like that to happen.

Yep. I remember when I was set up at the town fair. The two of them, they were walking from one table to the next, their arms around each other, always smiling like they had some kind of secret they were sharing. Sometimes they would stop to say somethin to one another, but instead of just sayin it, they would whisper it. Yep, they whispered quite a lot, those two. Never knew what to think of that. Made me suspicious sometimes. Maybe a little jealous, too—young love and all.

But sometimes, the two of them, they would kiss each other really hard for really long using their tongues, and they would do that right in front of the little children—I mean, right in front of them. I didn't like seeing that. Thought they shoulda had a little more decency, that's all.

But I'm sure they were good people once. I mean, I imagine he just snapped when she started dyin—or after she died, anyways.

Yep. Hurts to lose the woman ya love. Lord knows where I woulda ended up if my own woman croaked that young. Not here servin out ice cream cones, I reckon—no, sir.

Well. Anyways. That's all I got for y—ah, shoot. Sorry bout that. Guess I blabbered on for too long—it got all melted. Lemme get ya another cone. French vanilla it was, right? Want any of them sprinkles with it?

HOW MANY TIMES, Junior? How many times do I have to tell ya how to hold it? Ya hold it out like that and ya point it out like so. See that one grazin out there? Ya gotta point it out there, son. Ya gotta just take your time and point it out toward her there.

Nope. Not like this. Not like that, Junior. But like so. Hold it out there and point it there like so. Ain't fuckin rocket science, Junior. Any fuckin idiot can do it. Ya don't have to look it up in one of them books of yours, son. Ya just gotta point it out. Out where she's grazin, ya see? See where she's grazin? That's where ya wanna point it out at. See how I'm holdin mine? See where my hands are on it as I'm pointing it out there? Ya gotta hold it there firm, son. See how I'm holdin mine firm? Ya gotta hold yours firm, like so. Otherwise it will just flop out of your hands. If you're gunna keep holdin it like you're holdin it it's just gunna flop right out of your hands. See how I'm holdin it, son? See how I'm holdin it and pointing it and it ain't floppin? Ya see that?

Here, gimme that. Just let go a minute. Watch. Let me show ya. See how I'm now holdin yours? See how I'm holdin yours the way I'm holdin it? Now, I ain't pullin anything, ya see? No reason to get myself to pullin anything when I haven't even gotten to pointing it yet. It's all about how ya hold it first, son. Ya hold it steady first, like so, and once ya got it steady, you can aim it at her, like so. Don't even think about pullin anything yet. You're not ready to pull nothin yet. Just get the holdin it steady and gettin your aim down first and then we'll worry about pullin it later.

Here, ya can have it back. Give it another try. Now, put one hand there— yup. The other hand—that's it. Now steady it. Steady it, son. You're not steadying it. It's just floppin around there. Just floppin away.

Goddammit, Junior. How come you can't hold it steady? Ya know that boy down on the cow ranch yonder? Ya know who I'm talking bout? That little guy with the ears pointing out, like so? Well, that kid—he can hold it steady. He can hold it steady and point and goddammit, I swear, he's already pullin it. But you, here you are, not even a little boy like he is—not in years, anyways—and you can't even it hold it steady if your life depended on it.

Shit, son. I don't know what your mama and me did to deserve this. I'm just glad your granddaddy ain't around to see any of it, cuz if he were around, he'd be goddamned livid, I tell ya. Just goddamned livid. I mean, he's proba-bly watching all this from above like I'm watching you from where I'm standin here, scratchin his brains out tryin to figure out how he ever ended up with such an idiot boy for a grandson. I swear, it's moments like this I'm glad he's gone.

Now are ya gunna listen or are ya gunna listen?

Just put it down. Just put it down there, like so, on the ground there. There ya go. Now, turn this way. No, not that way—this way. Yup. Right. Now turn your shoulder, like so. Turn it—right. Now, plant your feet this way—see how I'm plantin mine the way I'm plantin them? Plant them this way. Like this way, goddammit. Right. Good. Now stay there. Just stay there. Here it is again. I'm gunna hand it to ya gently now, and I want ya to just hold it steady now. Just hold it steady and don't worry about nothin else. Got it there? Just hold it there steady now. Just hold it there steady. Steady it there, son. Steady it. Goddammit, Junior—how come ya still can't steady it even with me handin it right to ya there? What do I gotta do to get ya to hold it steady?

Tell ya what. I'm gunna get myself behind ya and reach over ya, like so. Just relax now, son. Just take a deep breath and relax. Don't think about nothin else and just watch how I'm gunna do this. See where I'm holdin it? Not holdin it here. Or here. Or there. But here. Right there. See that? Right there? Now, see how steady that is? See how I'm holdin it steady? Bend your knees a bit. Can ya bend them? A little more. A little bit more. Not that much. Good. That's perfect. Now let's steady it. See how it's steady now? See how it's not floppin around this way and that way like it was before? Good. Now let's aim it at her together. Let's you and me point it at her, like so. Good. How's that feel, son? Does it feel good? It should feel good to ya now. Now that we're here holdin it together the way we're holdin it, it should feel good. Does it feel good? Good. Now lean your head this way. Don't fight me, son. Just lean your head down this way. Down this way. This way, I said. No, not that way. This way. Your head should be here, ya see? Ya see that? See how I'm holdin your head where I'm holdin it like so? Just hold it there, son. Just hold it there steady now. Goddammit, Junior, just hold it there steady.

So, HERE's how ya would ride him, dear Grace. Take that hand of yours and put it here.

Okay, putting it there.

Alright, good. Now loosen that grip a bit.

Loosening.

Now—don't bend forward too much. Keep that back straight.

Straightening.

Good. Now put that other hand on the chest there, like so.

Right there?

A little lower.

There?

Little more toward the center.

There?

Yup. Ya got it. Now, what ya wanna do is ya wanna stroke that chest of his, let that horse know ya love him.

Like this?

A little more feelin.

This good?

Nope. More feelin.

How about that?

Yup. Perfect. Now, what's gunna happen is that you're gunna feel a rockin back and forth underneath ya as ya ride, and what ya wanna do is ride with it, not against it, so when ya start feelin that rockin feelin underneath ya there, you should start rockin your hips right along with it.

Like so?

Ha. Yes. Like so. That's it. Stay with her now. Now, when she picks up her speed, don't try to fight it, just ride along with the wave.

The wave?

Yup. The wave.

The wave.

Yes, love. The wave.

I like the wave.

Uh-huh. I like it too. Feel that wave get faster and faster now.

I feel it.

Feel it rise, higher and higher.

So high. So high.
Feel it grow, bigger and bigger.
Big. So big.
Feel it thicken, harder and harder.
Harder, yes, harder.
And warmer.
Warmer.
And deeper.
Deeper.
Inside ya.
Inside me.
Dear Grace.
Oh yes.
Dear Grace.
Say it again.
Dear Grace.
Say it again.
Dear Grace.
Oh love.
Dear Grace.
My love.
My Grace.
Our love.
Our Grace.
So much love.
So much Grace.
Deepest love.
Deepest Grace.
Always love.
Always Grace.
Forever love.
Forever Grace.
Eternal love.
Eternal Grace.
Oh.
God.
Yes.
Grace.

A MAN AND A WOMAN lie in drunken slumber in separate twin beds in an upstairs corner room of an old and creaky farmhouse. Their love for each other is no match for their love of drink and a good night sleep. The only dreams they dream are the broken kind. The room in which they sleep and dream is the very same one the man's father and mother slept in so many years ago. The man was their only child that ever lived past birth.

This man, this woman—this husband and wife who now live in the old and creaky farmhouse and sleep with broken dreams—they, too, have just one child.

A son.

A boy.

A boy with a crooked nose.

He is not asleep, this crooked-nosed boy. He is in the barn, alone with the horses and goats and pigs, a cigarette in one hand, an almost-empty bottle of jack in the other, sitting on a bale of hay. He utters words, sentences, out loud to himself—he is his own best company. This conversation with himself—it never ends well. Someone usually gets hurt in the end and more often than not it is he who gets hurt.

The only child.

The loner.

The mistake.

The byproduct of one night's careless, drunken ecstasy.

Having inflicted enough punishment on himself for the night, he gets up from his chair of straw, gives one of the horses a goodnight pat on the muzzle, and steps into the nighttime air.

It is a cold night. Too cold to be in just a tee-shirt and long johns. He looks out over the pasture, past the hills, where woodland creatures make their nightly noise, invisible, in the deep, dark forest. He gazes at the moon, its craters like eyeballs staring down at him, scrutinizing his every move and thought.

Fuck you too, the boy says to the moon, and flicks the cigarette behind him, the chilly breeze blowing it about, pushing its sparkling remains against the barn door, as the boy makes his way to the farmhouse, that old and creaky farmhouse, where a man he calls Pa and a woman he calls Mama, sleep in drunken stillness in the corner room upstairs.

On the other side of his eyelids, the man sleeping in the corner room sees two infernos, one for each eyelid. In one inferno, a stillborn child weeps. In the other inferno, an older voice, his father's voice, whispers Junior, Junior, Junior.

Junior, the man says, his eyes flickering open in the pitch-black room. He looks out the window. He opens it. He takes in a deep breath. The smoke creeps down into his lungs. A raging orange and red glow covers the barn.

Junior, he screams. The barn itself, its insides filled to the brim with all his precious livestock, scream the scream of burning children back at him.

Junior. The man runs onto the gravel driveway and stands next to the only child of his who ever lived. They watch everything they ever loved burn down into the earth.

Inside the farmhouse, up in the upstairs corner room where a hot breeze of smoke and soot blow through an open window, the woman still sleeps, her dreams already shattered long ago, her love for anything living buried under her own life's rubble.

Hold your horses, Grace. You're riding it too fast.

OUR BOY, she says. Some of the things he told me. About you. Makes me worry.

Her heart-shaped face, her elegant skin—they are of brownest complexion and almost as unblemished as that of her husband, save for a few freckles and acne scars on her chiseled cheekbones and unwrinkled forehead.

Is that so? Well, what's he sayin now? says the giant man, his glowing white face staring at hers across the long dining room table with nary an inkling of concern.

Says you've been touching him funny. Says you ain't hurtin him or nothin, but says it makes him feel strange—that you are no longer you anymore whenever you go on and touch him that way, that it's like you are someone else other than you.

The man with the glowing white face, the man who has had the city he governs under his powerful grip for nearly half a term, chews and gulps down the hunk of delicate rare meat in his mouth before responding to her thinly veiled inquiry.

And in what way is that?

Well, I'm not really—

In what way did he say I touched him? Tell me.

I'm not really sure. He didn't—

Come around and sit right here, the giant man says to his wife, shoving another morsel of meat with his silver fork into his enormous mouth. As he chews, his wife notices a single wet strand of spinach sticking to the corner of his mouth. The man's face is so very white that the green coloring of the strand looks more like dark red under the dim lighting of the room.

Sit right next to me here, love, he says, and show me what he showed you.

The slender brown woman rises slowly away from the table, her eyes watching her feet as she walks to the chair that her husband has pulled out for her next to him. When she reaches the chair, she carefully sits on its edge, still not looking at her husband's face, only at the floral patterns of her skirt flowing down her lap.

He continues to chew away at his dinner, the strand of spinach still moving in rhythm with his mouth. This time he does not wait for himself to swallow before speaking. Now, show me what he showed you.

Well, she says. He says you put your hand right here. She points to a spot on her lap.

Where?

There. Just showed you, didn't I? Said it was there.

No, no. Still in his chair, the giant man pushes himself out from the table, and tosses aside the linen napkin that covers only half the breadth of his lap. He faces her and puts two fingers under her chin so that she looks right into his large silver eyeballs and black eyelashes. The lashes, they flutter like wings of a flying insect toward her face, the strand clinging flat now on the side of his chin, like an exposed blood vessel, under the light.

No, that is not what I am asking of you, he says, his voice still calm, but rising in volume. What I want you to do is show me—on me, now—what he showed you when he said I touched him the way I touched him. So, show me. Show me where he said I touched him.

She cautiously moves one of her hands over her husband's lap without touching it and nudges two of her fingers in a rubbing motion back and forth.

Aw, come on now. He grabs her hand and places it right square on his groin. Now show me, darling. Show me the way our boy says I touch him.

She moves her fingers ever so slightly.

Come on now, darlin, he whispers. You can do it. You can show me.

She rubs her fingers back and forth on him. With her hands groping him reluctantly but intently, he lies back in his chair, his glowing face tilted up toward the chandelier, his big eyelids closed, the strand bobbing up and down as his mouth blows in and out.

Yes. Keep showin me. That's it. Keep showin me now.

She begins to weep, but she does not dare lift her hand away.

His giant body shudders in the chair, a moistness trickling through his trousers under her fingertips.

She begins to slowly pull away her hand, when he grabs her by the wrist with one of his giant clammy hands, then her privates with the other. He grits his teeth, biting his broad yet thin lip.

Is that what he showed ya? Is that what he showed ya on you? Did ya like it? Did ya? What difference does it make what I do to him if it feels good? I'm not hurtin him none. Only you are when you tell him that it's not right, that it's wrong. There is nothin wrong with it now, ya hear me? Nothin wrong at all.

But he's our boy, she says, tears streaming down the angles of her cheeks.

He's not my boy. He's your boy. He's brown like you, like his daddy. Not like me. He's your son, not mine. But he's still gotta follow my rules if he wants to live in my home.

He lets go of her wrists and cups his huge hand on the side of her face, strokes it gently, covering it entire. Now, you know I don't like to get angry. You know that about me, right? And there's no need for you to cry. What we got here, darlin. You. Me. The boy. It's beautiful. The people—they see us. They see the way we live and love. They aspire to be like us. So, what this is here—among the three of us—it's important. It's important for us to keep it going. For all of us to stick together. Cuz it brings hope. And joy. And possibility. To everyone in this city. Understand?

The giant man stands up, dabbing his trousers with the linen napkin, then tosses the napkin onto the seat of his now empty chair.

You tell the boy, if he wants me to, I'll stop. Tell him I'm terribly sorry if he does not desire my fatherly affections.

He turns away for a moment, but then turns back toward the woman, the strand of spinach now a jagged streak on his moonlike face.

But also let him know that I am deeply disappointed in him—that he broke our secret—and that I am not anyone else other than who I am.

IN A STALL of a barn, across from another stall where a lone mare watches in silence with pensive eyes, a man with a crooked nose and a woman with a crooked chin tug at each other's clothes until all that is left on their bodies is their washed-out underwear.

His are skimpy, with tiny holes where the fabric meets the waistband. Hers is a thong, with a faded bouquet of pink roses on the front.

This is weird, she says.

It is and it isn't, he says.

I never did this before.

Ya haven't? Ya mean that wasn't you all those times before?

No—you know what I'm saying. In front of something like that. She points her finger at the mare across from them.

He follows her finger. Ya mean to say you never did it in front of a horse before?

Um, yeah, she says. That's what I'm saying. But I suppose you have, right?

He shrugs his shoulders, and then moves his lips to utter the first white lie he can conjure up, but she puts a finger to his mouth.

I don't want to know, she says. Just take me and get it over with.

Well, since you put it that way, I think I'll pass.

She tugs him hard by the waistband onto the top of her fair skin. It's okay, she whispers in his ear. Let her watch. She sucks down on his lobe. Let's see if we can get a horse jealous.

His gray-blue eyes light up over her. I'll try to manage, he says.

The mare watches the lovers tussle and lock into one another, their eyes only for each other and never her own. With every sigh and grunt, with every whimper and moan, the mare whinnies ever so softly for the lust never quenched, for the heart never fulfilled.

THEY COME IN CARS and vans and pickups, a rickety caravan of smoldering engines, down the winding, dusty road that leads through an open white gate, passing a row of hickories on either side, snaking this way and that way over rocks and tree roots, until they reach the curving gravel driveway in front of the old and creaky farmhouse that sits fragile and beaten down next to the empty black pile of soot and ash that once formed the foundation of a barn older than the very town in which its owners hold residence.

A disheveled man in gray overalls, his teary eyes weathered from age and melancholy, steps down from the front porch of the farmhouse to greet the families who have arrived in a gesture of generosity and goodwill to construct a new barn for their downtrodden neighbor.

Barking and weaving this way and that around the man's legs is the farm-house dog, its thin black coat of hair covered only by the red bandana tied around its neck.

Thanks for coming, y'all, says the man, waving his shaky arm. Out of the vehicles come men with tool belts around their waists, women holding baskets and buckets of food and drink, and children of various size and age, some holding small items with anxious eagerness, others empty-handed and slumping along with indifference.

A sullen boy with a crooked nose, wearing a straw brimmed hat, and a red-and-white flannel tucked inside his dark blue jeans, looks about the visitors milling about his family's property, his gray-blue eyes tinged with deep longing and subtle shame. Small in stature, with his hands deemed too soft for manual labor by his rough-minded father, he stands helpless, listening to the jingling sound of metal coming from the tool-belted waists of the men and older boys, who only offer him the shortest of glances in his direction, oftentimes with the faintest of smirks.

I caused all this, he thinks to himself. While the thought racks him with remorse and weighs down on his wounded heart, he cannot help whiffing the air of opportunity that filters through the holes of his long and crooked nose.

Almost as fast as he breathes in this sense of hope and a new beginning, the opportunity takes its shape a few feet or so in front of him in the form of a girl with brown curls, wearing a light blue dress, ribboned in pink at the waist, like a Sunday churchgoer, holding a small wooden basket by the handle in one hand, and, in the other, the tiny hand of a much younger girl with blonde curls in a corresponding pink dress.

The boy on the porch looks up at the sky and then looks again at the taller girl in her blue dress: like an angel from the heavens, he says in his head. He sees her glance over her shoulder in his general direction, as if his very thought had been transmitted by airwave into her own brain.

As THE SUN starts to rise and as the wind taps gently against the window beyond her shoulder, a woman with green eyes and a crooked chin lies in bed, watching the bare and hairy chest of her lover rise and fall ever so subtly in the only remaining bed found in the old and creaky farmhouse they inhabit.

She tries to picture him inside her head, the way he was long before she ever laid eyes on him, from the day he was born, to the morning he found her, wet and desperate and alone, on a solitary bench in a city that began to feel less and less like home to her.

That nose. Oh, the sound it makes as he sleeps. And how wonderfully crooked it is. Was it a genetic mishap, as he seemed to imply it was, or was it just the way he was pushed or pulled from his mother's womb?

She tries to imagine what her lover would be like if he had been born a girl, but her mind keeps returning to her boyish images of him, for after all, in many respects, he still seems to be living in that carefree and desolate existence that characterized his youth.

And she is that way too, she knows. Still experiencing her life through the eyes and heart of a child. Still not fully free of her fear of abandonment, or her potential for abandoning others.

She strokes her belly. But she will not abandon this child. Nor the man-child still lying next to her, fast asleep, only moments away from learning about his latest rite of passage.

But what kind of father will this man-child be? She combs her fingers through his thick, wavy hair. A good father, the voice inside her head says. A good one—yes. One who will be as good to our child as he has been to me. One who will protect our new family and make it feel safe just as he has made me feel safe. He will not be like his own father. He will break the pattern. If I have to, I will help him break it.

With her head now on his chest, she listens to his heart beat and waits for his gray-blue eyes to open up wide and let the light in.

———— ⌁⌁⌁ ————

WHERE'S JUNIOR, says the disheveled man in the gray overalls. Anyone see my boy?

No one seems to listen to this man for whom they hammer and saw, drill and pound. With the men going about their building, the women and young children get the blankets and folding tables ready for the lunch break. Loaves of bread for sandwiches from one soft hand to the next. Cold cuts carefully laid out on tin trays. Water from wooden jugs poured into paper cups, the mothers gently admonishing their children to not spill, to not eat any of the food, to wait for their fathers and older brothers to come and sit with them so that everyone could eat together.

Junior. Goddammit, where the fuck is that boy at? mutters the host. The harsh and crude inflection of his voice startles the children and puts them on edge.

Junior.

Junior.

Junior.

Not a single person milling about his property replies. Not one. Not even the very boy who has been informally assigned this name the man calls out gives it any heed. With the pig of the same name having been burned down to a crispy pork chop by the flick of a finger, the boy with the crooked nose is now the only living creature on the property this coarse and crazed man could possibly be addressing. Not even the small and furry creature that the boy has cupped in his hands can claim that name for himself.

That mouse must be the cutest little mouse I ever did see, says the girl with the pretty brown curls in her hair. As they crouch closely across from one another in the tall grass behind the farmhouse, the boy wonders how old she is—she is a tad taller than he is—but then again most girls his age are taller than he.

You can pet him if ya want, says the boy. There, he says caressing its tiny head. Like that. You try.

Oh, I don't know, says the girl, with a coy grin. I don't want him to bite me.

Aw, he won't bite ya. I won't let him. Here. The boy takes her soft hand and places it on the mouse's head, and gently moves it back and forth.

Feels nice, don't it? he says. Their eyes meet. She bites her lip and smiles wide, her eyes sparkling.

Catching herself falling into the blue-grayness of his eyes, she pulls her hand away. Maybe we should go back to the others. They must be wonderin where we've been.

But don't ya wanna hold him? says the boy. Here, you can hold him. The boy holds out the mouse for her to take.

No, not right now. Maybe later. I think—

The boy pulls at the top of the girl's dress and lets the furry creature plop down toward where her pink ribbon hugs her at the waist in front.

She screams. She pulls at the dress until the mouse falls freely to the ground below her. The boy rocks this way and that way, holding his belly as he laughs.

Not funny, says the girl.

Sure it is.

Not.

Is.

She slaps him in the face.

He slaps her in the face right back and wrestles her to the ground.

A gunshot is fired.

The boy jumps to his feet.

Another gunshot.

A girl's name is called out into the summer afternoon air, its syllables being screeched at the highest of decibels, levels hitherto only associated with primitive beasts.

Get outta there, the voice screams. Get outta there off the grass. The voice contorts at such an animalistic pitch, it is hard for the boy to discern whether it belongs to a male or female.

It's my little sister, says the girl with the brown curls. The boy with the crooked nose, alarmed by the primal sounds and screams yet half-relieved that the screams and accompanying gunshots are not aimed at him, runs around the farmhouse, the girl trailing close behind, to learn the source of the commotion.

Run. Run this way. No, the other way. The other way. Get outta there.

The boy follows the screaming and yelling. The voices are both male and female, he discovers. A cacophony of competing screeches and shouts.

He looks out, over the fence, toward the pasture. A horse—a brown stallion—the sole survivor of the preceding weekend's barn fire, trots at a very slow yet methodical pace after a little girl in a pink dress. Every time she stops and looks behind her, the stallion stops. Every time she starts to run, the horse trots after her. To an outsider—and perhaps to this little girl giggling and running on the pasture—this might seem like harmless fun. A memory she will cherish for years to come. But for the onlookers screaming their insides out for the girl to return to safety, they know what will be the outcome if she is to continue her innocent cat-and-mouse game with the horse.

The screaming out of her name comes from so many of the visitors that they all seem to overlap each other, to cancel each other out, rendering their messages indistinguishable and indecipherable to the human ear, especially one belonging to someone as innocent as the little girl.

Another primal scream comes over the boy's shoulder, rattling his eardrum. He looks behind and sees the girl with the brown curls, the terror showing in her eyes.

She understands.

The boy understands.

So does the boy's father. He shoots his rifle in the air once again, but the horse does not respond.

Goddamn girl, the horse's disheveled owner says. What she gone about doing that for? Gunna get herself fuckin killed.

I'm gettin my gun from the truck, says one of the anxious onlookers, a burly man in thermals and jeans.

Dad, screams the girl with the brown curls.

The black farmhouse dog with the red bandana growls from the porch.

I wouldn't do that if I were you, says the horse's owner.

That's my youngest daughter out there, says the burly man. I'm not gunna just stand here and let her get trampled to death. If you're not gunna get your horse under control, then I will.

The disheveled man shoves his rifle sideways across the distraught father's chest to block him and pushes him back. You ain't killin my horse.

Get outta my way.

He's the only one I got left.

I said get the fuck outta my way, goddammit.

No sir, you get the fuck outta my way, or I will shoot ya right in your goddamn pie hole. This is my goddamn property. That is my goddamn horse. This is my goddamn—

The rifle flies out of the disheveled property owner's hands as the fist of the little girl's father strikes him flush in the jaw. The precision of his blow surprises its deliverer so, that it stops him in his tracks for a moment or two, enough time for the boy with the crooked nose to smack him across the back with a spare two-by-four, avenging the assault of his old man.

A woman among the onlooking crowd screams. So too does the girl with the brown curls.

Daddy, she cries.

The dog growls and jumps on and off the injured back of its owner's attacker.

This is all background noise to the boy. He knows what he must do and knows that time is short.

He picks up the rifle and rushes toward the fence. The little girl continues to run about the pasture, but from the subtle terror in her face, and with her giggling having subsided into gasps for breath, it seems she has slowly begun to grasp the gravity of her situation. As the boy hops over the fence, he sees the little girl fall to the ground, the horse trotting in her direction from several yards away, the little girl getting up but falling yet again, her tired little legs no longer strong enough for running. She rises off the ground once more and waits for the trotting horse, now galloping horse, the stallion now seizing on the weariness of its target, having made up its mind long ago to seek its own private revenge against the carelessness and recklessness of human youth. It charges faster and faster toward the child standing a few dozen yards in front of it, unaware that a boy holding his father's rifle aims to shoot it from behind.

The boy points the tip of the barrel at the sprinting horse and follows its advance toward the little girl. The rifle shakes in his sweaty hands, its length just shy of the vertical span of his small body.

Aim for the buttocks, Junior, bellows a familiar gruff voice from several yards behind him. Ya gotta hold it steady there and aim for the buttocks. The buttocks now, boy. Aim for the buttocks.

By the time the voice behind him has shouted the word buttocks for the fourth time in as many sentences, the boy has already fired his weapon, the charging beast dropping to the ground and sliding to a halt only a few feet in front of the shivering little girl in the pink dress.

A voice cries out the little girl's name. Just once. A woman's voice.

When the boy reaches the horse, he sees that it is still breathing. It kicks its three unwounded legs about this way and that, but the single wounded one is gushing blood, creating a deep, red puddle on the bright green grass.

The little girl shrieks.

The kicks get shorter and fewer.

The boy kneels down next to the horse, using one of his shaky hands to caress its black and silky mane. Just as his other hand begins to lay his weapon down on the ground, a seemingly invisible force yanks the rifle up out of his grasp.

Goddammit, Junior. I told ya to aim for the buttocks, didn't I? Not the legs, goddammit—the buttocks. Don't ya know your ass from your leg, boy? Now everybody here just step on back. Just go on and git. Gunna put this here bronco out of its goddamn misery.

A boy—one much taller than the one who shot his family's horse—comes running up toward the man with the rifle. Sir, he shouts.

Not now, son, says the man. Can't you see I'm tryin to give this poor animal some peace and quiet?

But it's your wife, sir. She's fallen out the winda.

Whoa, Grace. Whoa.

IN A BARN with no farm animals, save for a lone mare, a man with a crooked nose and a woman with a crooked chin lie still, dozing in each other's arms, against a bale of old hay. Inches from their feet, on the lookout for any sign of movement from the sleeping lovers, is a tiny black bug, no larger than the button on the woman's half-open blouse. It watches the woman's neck as her head lies on its side against the man's chest. It can see and smell the blood pulsating through the light purple vessels under her skin. More interesting to the tiny black bug, however, is the lumpy slab of flesh peeking out from between two shirt buttons where her belly lies in wait.

Something is brewing inside that belly, thinks the tiny bug. The freshest and purest blood, no doubt.

The tiny bug crawls stealthily forward, its eyes never wavering from its target. Onto the woman's canvas shoe it crawls, and then onto her ankle, resisting taking a bite as it moves its way all the way up her bare leg, traversing over her calf, the back of her knee, her thigh, her buttock, until it resurfaces for air through the tiny opening created between the lower slope of her back and the loose waistband of her panties. It sits there very still on the naked fair skin between shirt and panties, and rides the waves of its prey's respiratory rhythms until it feels its balance is steady enough to make its way back down inside the waistband, below the hip, over the upper thigh, into the groin, onto the outer edges of pubic hair, before pivoting back up onto her taut mound of belly flesh, where gurgling underneath is the purest cauldron of blood and membrane this bug has ever laid its mouth on. It takes a bite, then another, releasing its venomous saliva while never fully releasing its mouth from the fair flesh it has suctioned.

As sunlight retreats from the open barn door and the early evening air trickles in, a tiny purple ring forms near the center of the woman's belly where the bug has fully penetrated itself through her skin as well as into the membrane covering the half-formed creature incubating within. By the time the faintest of crescents has taken shape in the evening sky, the purple ring on the woman's belly mound has faded away almost as quickly as it had formed.

When the woman awakens and jostles her lover awake, she tells him the names she prefers if the child is a boy.

But what if it's a girl? he says.

It's not a girl, she says.

How do ya know?

I can tell from the way he kicks.

—⌘—

By the time the disheveled man with the rifle and his crooked-nosed son reach the front of the farmhouse, everyone who had been watching the drama unfold between the little girl and the brown stallion on the other side of the fence had already shifted over to an area of short dead grass and formed a circle three rows deep around the new focus of their attention.

Cummin through. Move outta the way. Lemme through now. Go on and git.

The butt of the disheveled man's rifle bumps a small girl in the back of the head, but the man pushes on through the crowd without flinching until he reaches his wife, his son following right behind him.

Dear Jesus.

He sees his wife stretched out on her back, just in front of the porch, one arm up straight over her head, the other reaching straight out at her side, forming a right angle with her shoulders. Her legs are positioned far apart from one another, like a scissor stuck in an open position. They appear stiff, her legs, locked by an unseen force, her tattered housedress pushed up close to her pelvis, enough to show the trim of her aged panties. Socks cover both her feet, but not shoes. One of her shoes is next to her where her face is turned, inches out of her reach, on the opposite side from where her husband and son stand observing her. Her eyes are wide open and bloodshot. With her face and arm aimed out to the side the way they are, it is as if she is trying to reach out for her shoe with her hand without moving a muscle in her body. Her body quivers ever so slightly and the soft whimpers from her mouth are barely audible.

A red puddle has formed around her fractured skull. It shines as bright as candy under the afternoon sun. The farmhouse dog, which has squirmed its way through the thick crowd of legs, licks at the puddle and then at the open wound in the woman's head.

Mama, whispers the boy. Mama.

He wants to scream the words, but his heavy breaths do not let him. He runs to her side and strokes her long, tangled hair. He pushes a strand away from her open mouth.

The husband of the deeply wounded stands weak and helpless, the rifle still in both hands in front of him. He looks down at the long piece of metal he holds and weighs his next move.

How'd it happen? one of them says.

Up there, another says. She points to the window above the roof of the front porch. She just came rollin on down that slope right there.

Nah, she wasn't rollin, says a new voice. More like a tumblin.

Anyone a doctor?

Somebody call a doctor.

Anyone know how to give mouth-to-mouth?

Someone better give it to her soon.

No one budges.

The man with the rifle knows what he would do if no one was here to witness it, and it would be the right thing to do, he thinks, no matter how it would look to anyone else.

The boy shakes his father out of his trance. Is Mama gunna die, Pa? Is she gunna?

The man looks over his shoulder, over the heads of his neighbors, to where his only remaining horse lies in utter stillness, a brownish heap on the greenest of grass, and then turns his face back toward the woman he stopped loving long ago.

With the sirens growing louder behind him, he watches as his wife receives mouth-to-mouth from one man after another.

THEY DON'T REALLY have a name for what you got—that's what I'm trying to tell you and your husband here. Or your boyfriend, I mean. This condition, it's been seen before—not in this hospital—but it's been seen, yes. But pinpointing an exact timeframe—I'm sorry, but that's something I can't give you. Three months, six months—could be nine months, a year even, for all we know. Whatever that timeframe is, we're well into this, so you should think in those terms.

The fetus—we'll see what we can do there. It won't be easy—that I won't lie to you about—but I think we have a decent shot with that. We've had ones born earlier here, much earlier, and we were able to come out on top with those, so, you know, we'll see what happens.

But since we don't know exactly how far along this situation is, my advice to the two of you—and this is friendly advice, not medical—but my advice to the two of you is to make the most out of the time you have together. Travel. Explore the world. Do the things you love doing best. Spend time with those you love most. Speak to people you haven't spoken to for a long time. Make amends. Bury the hatchet. Turn the page. But whatever you do, be smart. Don't do anything that would aggravate the condition. You know, like jumping out of airplanes or something. No rodeo rides, you hear? Keep yourself hydrated—drink lots of water. Bottled water, if you can. Stay out of the sun. Wear only long sleeve shirts, but keep it light. No need to bundle up unless it's the wintertime. Get plenty of rest—I know that sounds contradictory given what I just said about making the most of your time, but rest is important. You'll live longer if you rest longer. If things seem to be getting worse in a dramatic way, or if you're unsure about something, give us a call. We'll be here. Or at least one of us will be. I will tell you now that I will be on vacation for two weeks next month—my wife and I will be in the country, celebrating our twentieth. Anniversary, that is.

Say, don't you live in the country? Or that's just your husband here that does, right? I mean boyfriend—sorry again.

As far as medical marijuana goes, I don't approve. I mean, it's just no good, medically-speaking, for your condition. If you feel a need to binge, help yourself to a chocolate milkshake. Don't need to smoke to binge. And cigarettes—that's a big no-no. Like I said, I'm not so sure if your cigarette-smoking made this thing worse than it had to be—my guess is it didn't—but like I said, that habit would have caught up with you one way or another down the road. No need to shorten the time you have left any further. As your doctor, I advise more than ever to keep all facets of your life healthy though your impulse might be to do something drastic and carefree given your condition. Consider it a test of character. If you want to show the world what you're made of, why your life means something, the best way to do it is to keep everything healthy so that you'll give yourself enough time to show everyone what's what.

So. Be smart. Keep it healthy. Make the best of it.

Think that covers it all.

Did I cover it all?

Or am I missing something?

Yeah, I think that pretty much covers it all.

Well, in any event, less you have any more questions or concerns, I'd like to discuss financial matters and go over what this is all going to cost given your limited insurance coverage and lack of employment.

So, are there any more questions? Concerns? No? Good.

Let's move on to money then.

I GOTTA GO into town—need to talk to the banker about our situation here. You go sit with your mama and watch her. If she needs anything—water, medicine—just give it to her. Keep that rag wet—it'll keep the fever down. Try not to touch her though. Her wounds aren't infectious, but that fever of hers she's got now sure is.

The short boy with the crooked nose watches his graying, shaggy-faced father close the door of the bedroom in the upstairs corner of the farmhouse. He walks toward the window—the very same window his mother had tumbled out of—to watch his old man get into his rickety pickup, its ignition coughing the vehicle to life. The rusty, white heap of metal on wheels lumbers off the gravel driveway and winds its way slowly up the long and dusty road that cuts through the woods and continues on through to the main part of town.

The boy turns back toward the inside of his parents' bedroom, a room he has no recollection of ever finding himself in, save for a few very early boyhood instances in which the thunder in the sky crackled and shook the house so hard that he would run into this very room where his parents slept and would find some space for himself next to the still and unconscious body of his mother, the faint smell of cigarette smoke in her tangled hair and the bitter aroma of gin flowing from her mouth and nostrils as she snored gently into her dark and musty surroundings.

She would never open her eyes on those occasions, though sometimes he would see her lips move into the vaguest formation of a smile, and that acknowledgment of his presence, real or imagined, gave him enough comfort for him to nestle himself and fall asleep against the velvet cloth of her nightgown.

As he holds the wet rag to her forehead, he realizes he has probably seen his mother more with her eyes shut than open, exuding no awareness of his or his father's presence, her constant drunkenness and exhaustion always overtaking her petite and withering figure.

Why did she tie herself down to a man she did not love? Why did she throw herself at the other men—if those rumors were indeed true—when she could have lived a carefree life on her own without the burdens of marriage and motherhood? These questions and other thoughts like them spin around in the boy's head as he sits and watches his mother, bandaged from the eyebrows on up, wearing that same velvet nightgown that gave him such comfort and safety on those thunderous nights when he was such a small child.

He is still a small child. For his age anyhow.

After several minutes of holding the cold rag to her head, he lays it on the night table next to her twin bed, and strokes the back of his fingers against her cheek, then the other cheek, then her nose, and then, very gently, against the bandage over her forehead.

Her skin is hard and cold. He lowers his face to her lips and then tilts his head side sideways to listen and feel, but he already knows she is dead, perhaps having been so for some time now, perhaps well before his father's car ambled out the driveway, up the dusty road.

He sits on the bed next to his mother and imagines how he will tell his father. Hours go by before he awakens to the early daylight shining into the room, his small, fragile figure nestled one last time against the velvet of his mother's arm.

Lifting himself from the bed, he exits the room and walks down the stairs, calling for his old man, but gets no response. When he reaches the front door and steps onto the porch, he sees his father, slumped down in his wooden rocking chair, eyes closed, snoring heavily, fast asleep. The boy sits on the floor of the porch and watches this familiar yet strange figure in his life rock back and forth gently against the rhythm of the morning breeze, and waits for the man's eyes to open to his further degenerating reality.

---∾∘◡∘∾---

YET ANOTHER DOCTOR, he thinks. She looks too young to him to be any kind of doctor, never mind a doctor for a patient who is perhaps nearing the end of a foreshortened life.

Are you Grace's husband? Oops. I meant to say boyfriend. That's right— I think she had said that. Okay, well, she's out of intensive care now, but I would give the nurses about twenty minutes or so before going into see her— just so they can have enough time to set things up, okay? Now, we took a large sample out—we got in there deep. But just from the sonograms and from the excisions, we can see some visible evidence of spreading into the lungs, into the liver, into the large and small intestines. Her heart rate is now normal, but we can see some muscular trauma there, too. Whatever this thing is, it's proliferated and grown more intense. We have her on intravenous, and we'll be giving her painkillers whenever it's appropriate. We're now seeing a lot less blood in her cough, in her mucus, in her stool, but that could regress, so we should watch that. But there's a lot of muscle deterioration in both the upper and lower regions of her body—shoulders, arms, hands, legs. Her back, too, around the spinal cord, which is concerning, of course. My guess is she won't be on her feet for a while—or at least she shouldn't be. She should be getting all the rest she can get. And lots of water. She may not regain a full appetite for a few days, but she should still eat—even if it's just like applesauce or something soft like that.

The baby, says the man with the crooked nose. What about the baby?

The baby? You mean the fetus? Well, the fetus was removed, of course.

Is—is it still alive?

Um, alive? Well, I think the fetus had expired well before you got here. Think that was days ago, actually. Weren't you told that already? They were supposed to tell you that. Actually, this operation couldn't have taken place if there was a live fetus in there—it would have been too dangerous. But, yeah. The fetus didn't make it. I'm really sorry no one told you.

The man's knuckles curl underneath the brimmed hat he holds in his hands. Was it a boy?

Um, I'm not really sure. I'll check in on that and get back to you, if you like. I will say that it did not help your wife's—I mean, girlfriend's, sorry— situation that she was so well into her pregnancy when this all happened. But I will also tell you that the fetus may have created a buffer of sorts against the infection in terms of her own health and may have helped dilute some of the symptoms, so let's just hope for the best that she starts to recover a bit, that this thing, whatever it is, has stabilized, and maybe after a few days or so of keeping her here under our care, we'll have a better idea exactly what the source of the ailment is, maybe even have a name for it, which I know you and Grace have been wanting to know—understandably, of course. But I'm really sorry about that oversight in communication—you should've been told earlier. Unless maybe someone told her and not you, though I think she would have told you herself then, no?

I don't know, says the man. I'm not sure what she woulda told me.

Right. Well, even if she did know and didn't tell you, I wouldn't get too upset at her about it. She needs your support right now more than ever, and you're all she's got. I think your presence will be really important to her. I know she'll be very happy to see you. She says you were a horse-and-buggy driver and that's how you two met? So romantic. I love horses. I—are you okay there, sir?

The man hunches over in the waiting room chair and buries his head in his hands while the young doctor standing over him continues to talk over the ebb and flow of his thoughts.

He does not weep.

Are you able to follow what I'm saying? says the doctor.

The man lifts his head up and nods.

Okay, good. Well, again, sorry. Though, like I said, maybe it was a blessing in disguise.

What was?

The buffer. The fetus—it may have been a blessing.

A blessing, whispers the man.

Uh-huh. A blessing. Okay, so, I'll be back in a few hours or so with more info for you and your wi—oops. I almost said wife again. Duh. It's girlfriend, girlfriend. Alright, I have it down now. Okay? You take good care now. Stay strong.

SHE HAS NO friends, no family other than us, so, the way I see it, says the widower, there is no need to have a whole funeral for her.

The boy with the crooked nose listens to his old man and nods. His father uses words like mortuary and embalm—words he has never heard before in his short lifetime—and after two days of listening and nodding, the reverend arrives holding a single small book in his hand, followed by four men in black attire hoisting the long, wooden box from the back of a gray station wagon.

Your mama—she's in there, son, says the widower. He looks almost handsome in his worn and wrinkled black suit jacket and tie, his face now shaven. So, too, does the boy in the navy sweater his mother knitted long ago. Somehow, perhaps due to his slow physical growth, the sweater still fits him. It has always had a hole in the armpit, but no one has ever seemed to notice that except him.

The widower directs the visiting entourage to the side of the house where he has already dug a hole through the dead grass to bury the deceased. The boy hears his mother jostling inside the wooden box, as the men try to fit the unwieldy object into the hole. One of the men asserts that the hole is not large enough for the long, wooden box.

Oh bullshit, says the widower. I did the measurements just like ya says me to.

The men go back to the car and take out two shovels. Along with the benefit of a third shovel that the widower had left on the ground on top of a mound of dirt from his earlier digging, the men move quickly to expand the breadth of the hole. As they finish their digging, the reverend begins his eulogy, but the boy keeps his eye on the box. With the reverend's muffled language in the background, meaningless and empty words to his boyish ears, he imagines what a box for someone his size would look like.

His father leans over him and whispers. Any words you wanna say to your mama before they lower her in?

The boy looks up into his father's bloodshot eyes. The question makes his small body shudder. He wants to say something, but lacks the diction to say it.

It's okay, son, says the widower. Me neither.

THERE SOME THINGS you should know about me, Grace.

He looks at her slumped and naked body across the stall. It is hard to tell when she is awake anymore. She no longer looks like herself—she is more bone now than flesh—but he still loves her, still lusts for her.

He looks over at the mare watching him as he studies her. Don't you say nothin, Gracie. This is between me and her. Don't you spoil it for us now, ya hear?

His gaze returns to the bald-headed woman across from him, her skin dotted with red and purple spots, a blistery apparition of her former self. Her eyes open and close, but they no longer feel aimed at him, only at something distant and within, something only those whose lives have been cut short can see. She hears nothing, or, if she can hear, he determines, it seems that she can no longer distinguish the source of one sound from another.

She can no longer dress herself. The outfits he dresses her in are disheveled mish-mashes of wrinkled blouses and ragged pants, sometimes from his very own wardrobe.

In spite of all these circumstances, he continues to talk to her, to be with her, to confide and share with her.

He crawls to his beloved and clasps her hands in his, her head leaning on its side atop her shoulder. Grace, he says. Grace, my love. Can ya hear me? I know this is somethin you may not be able to feel in the way you were once able to feel it, but I need to do this, to feel this, for you and I, both of us, we are running out of time on this earth, and who knows what the next world brings for us sinners? I know we deserve a place in the kingdom of heaven— hell knows we earned it—but you and I, we are two lost souls who never got our fair shake, so why would anything in the next world bring us anything but the same? I need to remember, Grace. You may not look the same, but I know you are still the same woman underneath it all, the same woman I fell in love with that first mornin I found you alone and shiverin on a bench like a fresh baby out of her mama's womb, abandoned and tortured from the first breath onward. The same woman who said she never would in front of someone or something else, but then just went on and did it anyway cuz you knew it would make me happy. And no one ever tried to make me happy before. No one before you. And I'll never forget that, and I hope—I hope that I did some of the same for you, that I made you feel happy and loved the way you made me feel happy and loved. The way you accepted me for who I was, warts and all—a monster, at times, yes, but one to be pitied like the rest of us. We all have demons within ourselves, but you taught me—yes, it was you who taught me not to feel any shame about it, that it is not our own fault, nor is it someone else's, but just the cards we and those around us were dealt. I've tried to let go of this anger inside me—I know you've said I need to do that—but it just won't go away. It just keeps buildin and buildin no matter how hard I try to ignore it. I can't help feelin like I was cheated, like somethin I had wanted and finally had was taken from me before I had the chance to enjoy it to the fullest.

You.

Our child.

Our future together as a family.

And that's somethin—goddammit, Grace—that's somethin I just can't put behind and bury in the dirt. Cuz if I buried it, if I just let it go like I know ya want me to—well, it just wouldn't be right now, would it? No, siree, it sure wouldn't.

I gotta make this right, Grace. For your sake and mine, and for our child who never was given the chance—I gotta make this right.

But I want you to know, Grace, that whatever happens I'll be okay, that sometimes it's just the act that counts and not what's achieved. It's about the doing and not the consequences of doing, is what I'm sayin here, I guess.

Sometimes I look in your eyes now and wonder if you still hear me, or if you can even feel my hand touch your hand the way it is now, or my lips push against your own. But maybe the same goes for there too—it's more about the act itself than what it achieves.

What's that, Grace? Peace of mind. Yup. Ya just hit the nail on the head, yessiree. Maybe that's what I'm going for here—that peace of mind everyone talks about but never really gets for themselves.

Yup.

Right.

Well, we can discuss more of that peace-of-mind stuff later. Like I said, the clock's tickin loud and clear for the both of us, so it's best we now get started. So, here—let me help ya outta them clothes.

After stripping his beloved down to her panties, he reaches into the waistband of his trousers for his flask—the one he had hid from her for so many months—and takes a swig. The inside of the old tin can is so full of rust he can taste it in every sip, but he has grown used to the flavor, and he has never been one to care much about the color of his teeth, nor what sort of residue is stuck between them.

Shut up, Gracie, says the drunken man. He hurls the old hunk of metal at the mare, just missing the top of her head. I don't wanna hear another sound out of ya, ya hear? Not one.

He turns back toward the dying woman slumped against the wall. He begins to remove her panties, but sees the droplet of red dribbling down the corner of one of her eyes, stopping him in his tracks.

The clock, he says. It's tickin faster than I thought.

He gets up off the ground and enters the stall across where the mare now stands calm, almost catatonic. He grabs the stool behind her, gets up on its top step, and begins to undo his trousers.

Brace yourself, Grace. This is me at my most undignified.

Mare.
   Mayor.
   Mare.
   Mayor.

A SMALL BOY with a crooked nose watches his father, an overall-wearing heap of bony flesh and bloodshot eyeballs, point a cattle prod at a tired, old mare in front of them with the disposition and efficacy of a grammar school teacher.

Okay, son: What do ya call this?

Her muzzle.

Right. What do you call this?

Her cheek.

Yup. Good, good. Now, what do you call this area here?

Her throatlatch.

And this area?

Her neck.

Uh-huh. And what do ya call this right here?

Her shoulder.

And this area?

Her breast.

And this little thing here?

Her point of shoulder.

Right. And what's this thing called under here?

Her jaw.

Yup. Yup. And that?

Her forehead.

And that?

Her.

Her what?

Her.

What is it—her what?

Her poll?

You got it. And this?

Her crest.

And this?

Her withers.

And that?

Her back.

And what's this area here?

Her point of hip.

Good. Good. And this here?
Her ribs—no, I mean her flank.
Okay, good. Now what are these?
Her ribs.
Right. And down here?
Her belly.
Here?
Her girth.
Good job. And this?
Her forearm.
Uh-huh. And this?
Her cannon?
Her what?
Her cannon bone?
Nope. Take another guess.
Um, her. Her. Her.
Her chestnut. Got it now? Okay, next: What's that right there?
Her knee.
And that?
Uh—her cannon.
Right. Good. And that?
Her coronet band.
And that, of course, is?
Her hoof.
Right. Okay. Let's see here now. Okay, what's that right over there?
Her. Her hock.
And that?
Her gaskin?
Her gaskin? Well, are ya gaskin me or tellin me, son?
Um. Tellin.
Yup. Okay then. Now what's that here?
Her thigh.
Right. And what do we call this?
Her buttock.
Yes, sir. Yes, sir. And this?
Her. Her, um. Her.
Remember: it's not a dick and it's not a cock, it's a. . .
Dock.
Bingo. And that area above it right there?
Her croup.

Very good. Very good. And now for the important parts. What's this?

Her stifle.

Yup. And this beautiful thing?

Her sheath.

Her what?

Her sheath?

Her sheath? What is she a goddamn she-male? What's that called right there?

Um. Um. I don't know. I forget.

You forget, eh? You forgettin the most important part of her now? Come on now, Junior. Get down here with me.

The man pokes at the folds underneath the mare, twirling them at the tip of his cattle prod.

Alright now, Junior. See that gorgeous thing right there? That thing there is called an udder. Ya know, like a cow has an udder? These mares—they got dem too, see that? Beautiful, right? Right. So don't forget that now, ya hear?

Okay.

Good. Now there's one more thing I haven't showed ya yet, but I'm gunna show ya now.

The man gets behind the mare, the boy in tow. He takes the prod and pushes the tail up with its tip.

See that thing there? Ya know what that is, son?

The boy looks and knows, but shrugs his shoulders up and down regardless.

Oh, come on now, Junior. Ya know what it is, so say it.

It's her. It's her.

Her what? Say it.

Her anus?

Her anus? Is that what ya call it now? Her anus? Goddammit, Junior—what are ya, some goddamn choirboy? A preacher's son? Anus. Jeez, son. How about her asshole—does that work for ya? Or better yet, how about her gloryhole? I think that sounds better: her gloryhole. But ya know what I like to call it, son?

The boy shakes his head and watches the twinkle in his father's weary eyes.

I like to call it her bullseye. Come on over now right here and I'll show ya why.

CAN SOMEONE turn it off? Can someone come in here and turn it off? Hello? Anyone? Anyone out there who can come in here and turn it off?

The man with the crooked nose pokes his head out the door, but no one is there to come in and turn it off for him. No one cares about him and his crooked nose. They are too busy watching it themselves on the screen that is turned on in their station area to care about someone like him who wants them to come in and turn it off for him.

Besides, who wants to come in and turn it off for him when the Great Savior of the City is addressing them directly over the airwaves with another solemn proclamation?

No, they are too captivated by their city's hero, with his massive head glowing like the brightest of moons under the camera lights and his colossal mouth issuing forth yet another benevolent decree, to be distracted by a short man with a long, crooked nose.

After all, who cares about a short man with a long, crooked nose asking them to come into the room where his beloved lies barely conscious—exhausted from unspeakable pain and suffering, her skin blistering in some areas, festering in others—so that they could come in and turn it off for him? And who cares if this short man with the long, crooked nose is watching her like a hawk, fearing the next blink of her eye, the next breath from her lips, will be her last?

No, they would not be distracted.

No, they would not come in and turn it off.

With those elegant eyelashes fluttering about on the screen, how could they ever come in and do such a thing?

Even the man with the crooked nose can see how elegant those eyelashes are as they flutter about on the screen. So elegant are those eyelashes that it hurts his insides to think of them so elegant.

By the time the hallowed mayor finishes delivering his latest edict, and as the image on the screen switches to a dog hovering over an empty bowl, the man with the crooked nose, who has all but forgotten what he has asked the nurses to come in and do, turns to his beloved who lies silent and motionless on the hospital bed beside him, and realizes that he has missed her last blink, her last breath.

He lets go of her hand and glares at the screen, gritting his teeth.

It is now blank, the screen.

Someone has turned it off.

Someone has turned it off without even ever having to come into the room to turn it off.

―――――⊶⊰✿⊱⊷―――――

A MARE SLEEPS in its stall, standing up on all four of its legs, unaware of the tiny eight-legged black creature who has crawled up from its front hoof, up past its pastern, its fetlock, its cannon, its knee, its forearm, and now sits still and watchful from its breast, catching its own breath from the long trek it has made from the undercrust of the earth, waiting for the right moment to sink its venom into the part of the horse that is its juiciest: the jugular groove.

And the throatlatch would make for a tasty dessert, would it not?

And what about the fleshy man who sleeps in the corner of this horse's stall, his naked skin uncovered and unprotected, his fluids oozing out from all his bodily holes, the aroma of his alcoholic blood, his nocturnal defecation, filling the air all about him—would he not also make a worthwhile host?

Of course, he would. Of course. But with the mare's jugular just in reach, the carnivorous crawler has already made up its mind: eat from the horse.

The tiny creature raises its tiny leg to make its move, to pounce, to strike, to bite down, to suck out, when the horse's body suddenly trembles and jerks up—just a random tic of muscle and nerve—causing the bloodthirsty insect to run for cover, for it fears that its sneak attack has been foiled.

But it has not been foiled. The mare returns to its silent stillness. The tiny nightcrawler regains its bearings and finds itself at the base of its target's mane. It takes a careful step into its silky thickness, crawling up, through, and around its many strands like a child walking in an uphill forest. On the way, the tiny black creature runs into something similar to itself, only larger, browner and no longer alive—perhaps a fallen victim of a failed offensive. It gives the tiny black crawler pause, but it remains resolute, determined to follow through on its mission, to reach the jugular, even if has to be reached from an alternative route. It crawls up the mane, weaving its way upward along the twists and turns of giant hair follicles, pushing its way through their almost suffocating density, until it reaches the mane's uppermost end, veers around the curvature of the mare's head, and reaches an enormous cavity it had not ever considered having to encounter when it first embarked on this arduous expedition to its next meal: the horse's ear.

The tiny black bug stops to reflect. The jugular lies in wait just inches below, but the cavernous hole beckons. What luxurious riches must lie in the hole's innermost depths. Would it not be worth pushing on a bit farther for something greater, for something larger, for something more satisfying than any crawler of the night could imagine? The tiny black creature can smell the blood pumping through the outer vessels of the horse's ear, hear the infinite bloodstreams gurgling deep from within. The prospects that lie within its reach, their overwhelming promise, make the tiny bug quiver with awe, but they do not deter it from its huge undertaking.

The determined little creature takes a deep breath, then exhales. It reaches out with its front leg onto the rim of the giant ear, and squirms and wriggles the rest of its body upward until it sits firmly on that first fleshy ridge on the dark and slippery path to the unknown.

The mare continues to sleep and dream, on the cusp of awakening to a world without sound.

---⊰∘⟠∘⊱---

He is to bury her ashes under the hickory tree behind the farmhouse on the anniversary of the day they met—that was her request—the very same tree under which they made love on various occasions, including the very first. He gets as far as carrying the urn out to the back of the farmhouse, but the wind is too strong, so he returns to the house, places the urn back on the mantel above the hearth, and waits for the wind to dissipate.

He waits for several minutes, his attention alternating between the urn and the window, and then decides to take another shot behind the house.

Let's give it another go, Grace.

He reaches the tree and crouches down on the ground. He holds a fallen leaf in the air, and releases it, watching it float past the tree into the tall, brown grass beyond before ever landing.

Fuck you, wind.

The man with the crooked nose stomps back toward the house, up the porch, through the screen door, places the urn back on the mantel, and sits himself back down into his favorite chair, a decades-old recliner with a hole the size of a watermelon in the back. He falls into a deep slumber, as the living room window rattles with the late morning wind. By the time he wakes up again, the sun has sunk below tree-level, the wind now gusting against the window even harder.

He looks at the urn on the mantel.

Grace.

Gracie.

He had not fed the mare all day.

He walks out the front door again, this time toward the barn, the harsh wind blowing against his face. When he opens the barn door, the mare, having lain down on its side for most of the day, spent from ravenous exhaustion, jumps to its feet, whinnying and bucking its head up and down like a bronco gone deranged.

There, there, Gracie girl. Let me get them oats out for ya.

When he reaches for the pail of oats, he sees there is not enough for even a quarter of a normal portion.

He feeds what is left to the mare, knowing that will not be enough, and when the mare reaches the bottom of the pail, he strokes her muzzle and tries to calm her expectations, for he knows that the stores in town that sell horse feed are closed until morning.

But the mare refuses to wait, her legs kicking against the walls of her stall, her whinnying reaching a feverish pitch.

I'm sorry, Gracie, but you're just gunna have to sleep on it.

The man with the crooked nose opens the barn door, the wind's gust shutting it behind him and pushing him back toward the farmhouse as if it were some giant, invisible hand guiding him by force to some predetermined destination.

When he gets inside the house, he heads straight back to the living room, sits himself back down on the recliner, grabs the flask atop the adjacent side table, and begins his nightly binge. Halfway through the flask, his eyes lock back on the urn above the mantel, the tiny container barely visible now in the darkened room.

Cheers, Grace. Lord knows I tried.

He takes a long swig back into his throat, all but emptying what remains inside the flask, then releases a deep sigh, realizing no amount of hard drink will squelch his feeling of defeat.

Grace. Grace. Grace.

Gracie.

It hits him like a thunderclap, his body shooting up from the old recliner and hurling toward the mantel where the urn sits undisturbed in its quiet majesty. He grabs the urn and marches out the door, convinced that his beloved has delivered a message to him from within the urn's confines, the wind blowing furiously against his diminutive figure, as if trying to ward him off from achieving his mission. He holds the urn close to his gut, guarding it from danger, protecting her, his beloved, from being further obliterated from existence.

After a long tug-of-war with the wind, he yanks open the door of the barn and heads right to the back corner where the mare is still kicking her legs against the walls of her stall, her hunger having driven her into an even more enraged state of madness.

Gracie. Gracie. She spoke to me, Gracie. My beloved—she spoke to me. She's right here, Gracie. Right here in my hands here. She wants to live on inside you, yessir. I know, it sounds crazy, Gracie, and I know I've been wrong about certain things in my life, but this thing—this is a real thing, this thing. Ya see, Gracie, what she wants ya to do is eat what's left of her so she can live on inside you. She wants you to eat what's left of her so she and I can still be together, ya see? Ya know, so she and I can be together for that much longer, ya catch me? The wind, me oversleeping, you not having enough oats to eat—it's all her doing, Gracie, I swear it. She needs ya, Gracie. She and I—we need ya. We need ya to eat this. All of it. All of her. So, please, Gracie, please do this for us. I swear I'll be a better man to ya. I'll go into town first thing in the morning tomorrow and buy up all the oats in the goddamn county if you just do this one thing, Gracie. Just this one thing.

With nary a protest, the starving mare devours the exotic supper, the frenzied effect of the insane man having unnerved her enough to not solicit a second serving, then retreats to the back corner of the stable as the man with the crooked nose observes her with wild new eyes, watching for any inkling of his beloved inside the mare's form.

Now DON'T GO tellin Mama what you saw here, Junior. Let's just keep this between you, me and the horse here. Believe you me, if there was anything really at all wrong with what I've done, I wouldn't stop ya none from going on off and tellin her exactly what you saw, but believe you me, it's just one of them things that looks worse than it really is, yessir. In fact, maybe when you're a bit older, I'll teach ya how to do it yourself. But right now, don't get any bad ideas, cuz this sort of thing what ya just saw with me and the horse right here—that ain't for little youngsters like yourself to, uh—what's the word I'm lookin for?—engage in.

Ya see, this horse right here—she smart in some ways, but not so smart in others. I mean, if ya think about it a little bit, it's kind of just like how us people are: we too are smart in some ways but not so much in others. But this horse right here—well, all our horses, for that matter—they don't know what it was I was doing there with this horse right here. Or, maybe they do, but they don't understand what grown-ups call implications, ya see. They just kind of sit there and eat grass or whatever they feel like putting in their mouths. For them, it's just more about doing things to stay alive—like eatin grass and drinkin water. They don't have to deal with the desires that get in the way and muss things up in their lives the way people have to. They don't worry about money or pleasin the missus or even takin a bath, for that matter. I mean, do ya even think for a second that this mare right here even cares how she smells? Hell no. For her, it's all about the next meal and the one after that.

I guess in some ways, that's what I try to do for you, me and your mama— I'm thinkin about our next meal, about keepin up our home, our family. But when you're a man like I am—which you will grow up to be someday—there are a lot of these unwanted desires in the way that trip ya up on what ya wanna get out of life, what ya wanna get for your family, ya catch me?

Oh, you'll see for yourself someday, yessir. You're probably sittin there thinkin the world is a straightforward place, but you'll learn sooner or later that it isn't. And maybe you seeing me with this here mare here the way you just saw me with her is your first glimpse that this life is not as straightforward and cut-and-dry as you might have once thought. There's no real bad in this world. But there's no real good in it neither. And what's tragic about that is unlike dem horses that we have here on the farm, we let it get to us. Cuz

86

believe me, I know, the thing you just saw with me and this here horse right here—that got to ya just the way it gets to me as I stand in front of ya here having to explain it to ya.

But I wanna tell ya somethin, son—and I'm gunna say this cuz you're my boy and I know ya got some of me in you whether you like it or not. Okay, here it is: don't worry about what others think of ya or what they'd think of ya if they were to know everything about ya. It's easier said than done, yessir, but the more ya remind yourself of that the easier it will be to forgive yourself, and the easier it is to forgive yourself, the easier it will be to forgive others. And it takes a real man to do that—to forgive others as well as yourself—but, I'll tell ya this, it's the only way to live, son, the only way.

Heck, I know I drink too much. No one needs to tell me that. I know what everyone is sayin about me around town. Don't think for a minute that I don't know, cuz believe you me, I know. I know. I know. I know. And I know it must be rough on ya, son, having to hear what people say about your ole pa, never mind your mama. But I know my limitations. I know my vices. I know the errors of my ways. Not everyone sees that in themselves, but I see it in myself, yessir. And ya know what? And goddammit, Junior, do you wanna know what? I forgive myself for it. And cuz I forgive myself for it, I can forgive you and your mama for your sometimes—okay, here it goes— sinful ways. Think I don't know about your mama and the men at the tavern? Think I don't know what you're doing, son, when I hear that bed of yours go squeak-squeak in the night when I come up the stairs? I know exactly what you're doing, and I can probably imagine what you're thinkin too when you're going at it the way you're going at it cuz, believe you me, I've thought of the same thing in my own head when I was a young boy, yessir.

But, son—son, it's important that ya listen to me when I say this to ya: it's not your fault. Ya hear? It ain't your fault doing what you do up in that bedroom of yours just as it ain't my fault what I just did with this mare right here. And, yes, while I know it probably still ain't all right to do what I just did with her, knowin me, I'll probably go off doing it again sometime somewhere down the road. And ya know what? I'm okay with that—yessir, I am.

Son—ya know what, son? In a weird sort of way I'm glad you saw what you saw cuz now you've learned something about your old man, about your-self, and about how the world works.

Yup, I said it: I'm glad.

But having said what I said, your mama—she's a sensitive one, and we know how she can get about certain things. Ya see, women are a little different when it comes to understandin or not understandin certain things—but that's a whole other discussion that we can have at a later date. But being that she is the sensitive type, I truly think it best if we kept what happened here, or what you saw happen here, between just you and me—or you and me and the horse here, anyway.

Hey, speaking of horses: our horse in question—I noticed she smelled a little funny. Would ya mind washing her up before heading back into the house? I think the bucket is over in the corner where the hose is.

I appreciate it, son. Good talking with ya. Glad we had this discussion.

THE PROBLEM is finding the right size.

He grabs one of the wooden chairs from the farmhouse kitchen and carries it over to the barn. He places it on the ground behind the horse and gets himself up on it.

Too high.

He gets down from the wooden chair, carries it back to the house, picks up one of the small chairs from the family room, and heads back to the barn.

Close, but not close enough—still a little too high.

The mare's tail twitches back and forth, tickling his knees. He likes the way it feels—makes him giggle a bit—but the situation is just not practical enough.

He heads back to the house, grabs two more chairs—one from his parents' old bedroom, one from the guestroom. They seem lower to the ground to him.

These might work, he thinks.

He carries them to the barn, one in each hand, the sun beating on his crooked nose and sweat dripping from his brow. His armpits feel moist and sticky. He has not bathed in days. All his crevices itch.

He places the two chairs behind the mare and stands on one, then the other.

But neither work well. One is too low—he would have to stand on his toes to make it right, and he preferred not to have to do that—and the other is about right, but too unsteady.

He paces back and forth in the barn for several minutes, mulling his next move.

Maybe I should try that old night table that's in the attic, he thinks to himself. It would be a bitch to carry down all those stairs, but it would be worth the reward.

He climbs all the way up the stairs of the farmhouse and enters the musty corridor of the attic. On the walls are old black and white pictures—ancestors he never met, mostly. When he reaches the end of the corridor, he enters the only room on the floor.

An old pool table. A broken-down grand piano. A freestanding mirror. A wooden chest. Tall rectangles wrapped in paper, leaning against the walls everywhere—paintings, most likely. And back there in the corner, hidden behind an antique dresser, is the old night table, its pinewood surface covered in a thick coat of sawdust, its bronze legs tangled in cobwebs. He imagines it being just right for the occasion, but he is too afraid of spiders to even go near it.

He looks back at the wooden chest. Leaning up against it is a steel step stool, folded up. He unfolds the dusty stool and stands on its top step.

This is it, he thinks. This is the one.

He thrusts his hips this way and that way, a spasmodic street mime without an audience.

Yessir, it would work.

He tries to catch a glimpse of himself in the freestanding mirror right in front of him, but it is covered in too much dust.

He imagines what he would look like in the mirror, the middle of his body rocking back and forth. He thrusts harder and harder until the stool's legs give way under him, sending him crashing to the floor.

No, it would not work. Not steady enough.

The resolution to his problem, he concludes, is not in this room. He sits himself up on the floor, dust still rising up all over him from his fall.

I'll have to build it myself, he says to himself.

He walks all the way down the stairs of the house, back into the family room, through a door that enters right into the garage, where a rusted-out, half-century-old flatbed sits idle. Squeezing his small body in between the front of the car and the wall, he makes it to the far side of the garage. He opens and closes several small drawers of old tools and construction ware until he finds what he is looking for: measuring tape.

When he makes it back to the barn, his horse is standing just where she had been. She seems so still to him at times, that it sometimes worries him. He is not sure if it is a consequence of her transformation into his beloved or just her hearing having gone to shit.

Can a horse die on its feet?

She blinks her eyes twice, snaps her tail once.

More a moving sculpture than a living horse, it sometimes seems to him.

He walks behind her once more, runs the tape down from the top of her tail, and subtracts an inch or so from this measurement. One of her hind legs, he remembers, is longer than the other, and though that concerns him a bit, he knows that this is not as important as where the top of the tail is. He measures from his own pelvis to the floor and then runs the calculations.

He is good at math.

HELLO? GRACE? Can ya still hear me, Grace? Are ya still in there?
Neigh twice if you're still in there.

THE SIGN on the front door of the hardware store reads OPEN EVERY DAY ACCEPT SUNDAY. The store's clerk—who, no doubt, is the author of this misspelled sign—is perhaps not the brightest of men, but he is the best hope for what is needed.

What is it ya need, exactly? the clerk says. He is older than the man with the crooked nose across the counter from him, but perhaps not as old as his wrinkled and weathered skin would suggest. He reeks of cigarette smoke. His bespectacled eyes are so narrow that it is tough to see the grayness of the eyeballs inside them.

I need one of those, says the customer. He points to the row of saws hanging from hooks on the wall behind the clerk. At the end of the row of saws is a small television set mounted high up on the wall. The local news is on, closed-captioned.

Which one you want? says the clerk. We got lots of them.

That one, says the customer. Or, I don't know, maybe that one.

That one or that one?

Yup.

What ya gunna do with it?

Gunna cut me some wood with it, yessir.

Well, I reckon that. But what I mean is, what are ya tryin to make with it?

A box.

A box? Ya mean, to put things in?

The customer turns his gaze from the row of saws to the clerk, who is still looking up at the wall, admiring his collection.

No. It's gunna be a box that I could stand on.

Ya mean, like a step stool to step up on?

No, I mean like a box to step up on.

Ya mean, like a crate?

No, I mean like a box.

The clerk finally turns back toward his customer across the counter, giving him one of those looks just shy of suspicion.

Okay then. But what good will it do ya just standin on it? We got some rope if ya need some of that, too.

The clerk bursts out cackling at his own dark joke, but the customer with the crooked nose is not amused.

I don't need no rope. Just one of them saws ya got hangin there.

Oh, I know, I know. Was just joshin ya, that's all. Never hurts to ask though, does it? So, just a saw, eh? For a box for standin yourself on and nothin else. Well, in that case, this one should do.

The clerk steps up onto a steel step stool. The counter he stands behind is nothing else but a counter, with no display case attached in front of it, allowing the customer with the crooked nose to see the stool in its entirety. He is surprised to see how well the old man balances himself on the stool as he leans toward the wall to retrieve the saw.

The clerk steps down from the stool. Will that be all, junior? Need any nails, screws, bolts—anything like that?

Did you just call me Junior?

The clerk looks at the customer with the crooked nose, half-smiling and only half-aware that perhaps some line has been crossed.

Well, yes, I did.

Why did ya call me that?

Well, I don't know. I guess I felt ya look young enough to me to be called junior, that's all. Did I say somethin wrong? I mean, I meant no offense or nothin. I was just—

You were just what?

Thinkin ya look young enough, that's all.

The customer with the crooked nose reaches into the pocket of his trousers for his wallet. Looking up at the television screen, he sees the city mayor speaking from the podium with families-first earnestness. He watches the black tickertape crawl calmly across the screen sideways as he speaks. The tiny white letters are too small for him to read.

Will that be all, sir? Need any nails, screws, bolts—anything like that?

No. No thanks.

Ya sure now?

Yessir. Thanks.

Okay then. That'll be—

And I'll take that stool you were using there, too.

Sir?

How much is it?

How much is what?

The stool.

The stool?

The one you were just standin on there.

Well, this one here is not for sale, but I got me plenty of others just the same in the back, if ya have a minute.

I have just one, I'm afraid.

Okay then. Be back in one minute.

On the television screen, men and women stand up from their chairs and applaud the giant man behind the podium. The mayor raises his enormous hand and waves it in the customary farewell of his trade.

A YOUNG BOY with skin as brown as earth lies on his bed, as his mother strokes his thick, african hair, her thin fingers caressing his small and fragile scalp.

Why do we stay here? he says to his mother.

Cuz right now we have to, says the woman with the chiseled cheekbones and skin as brown as his own. If we try to leave, he, his men—they'll find us, and then things—well, they will only get worse for you and me.

You're afraid of him?

Yes, I am. I am afraid of him.

Do ya love him?

I loved the man I thought he was. I loved the man that other people think he is.

Did ya love my real dad?

I barely knew your real dad.

What was he like?

Well, I'm not really sure. Seemed like a nice man. But I barely knew him.

Where do ya think he is now?

In heaven.

Was he buried somewhere near here or was he buried where he was killed?

Who told you he was killed? Don't use that word around here. How he died—it was an accident.

Like a car accident?

Well, there was a car—yes, I guess you can say it was like a car accident.

So they buried him where the accident was—in another country?

No. He was buried here. Just outside the city. With his family.

But we're his family.

No, love. This here—you and me—that's our family.

And Dad?

What about him?

Is he part of our family?

The woman with the chiseled cheekbones locks eyes with her son. His are of the same chestnut hue as her own, but his flattish nose and squarish chin are of the same mold as those of his real father, she thinks.

Why don't you just get some rest, love? We can talk more about this another time. You should get some sleep. ·

Will he touch me again?

He won't touch you again. I promise.

I wish I could see my real dad.

I wish you could too. But he's watching over you. He sees you.

But he can't stop him.

The woman's eyes turn watery. She was once a child too—a victim in her own right—but she holds firm. Please, love. It's time to go to bed. Now go ahead and get yourself under the covers. Go on now.

We need to get out of here, Mama.

We will, love.

We need to get out of here now.

Soon, love. Soon.

Okay, junior—I mean, sir, I mean. Here's what I got.

The clerk lays down the folded-up stool on the counter for his eager customer with the crooked nose to see.

What's that? says the customer.

The step stool. Ya said ya wanted one, didn't ya?

I said I wanted one like that one there.

Well, it is like that one there—just a different finish, that's all.

Show me.

Show ya?

Show me it's the same.

Show ya it's the same?

Yessir, show me. Stand up on it now and show me it's as steady as the one you were standin on there.

Now, look, sir—

Show me.

Hearing the intensity behind the customer's request, the clerk obliges. He wants no part of any trouble. Just wouldn't be worth it over a damn stool.

Fine, I'll get up then and show ya. He unfolds the stool, sets it to the ground, and gets up on its top step with the same amount of ease and steadiness as with his own stool.

Ya happy now? says the clerk.

Push your hips forward.

What's that?

I said push your hips forward. Thrust them forward. Like so.

Hey, is this some kind of joke, mister?

Thrust them. This is no joke. Thrust them. Like so.

The clerk stares with squinted eyes down at the short man with the crooked nose standing below. He can sense the insanity from across the counter. No point in pissing the fella off. Just get it over with and get out of this clean.

The clerk thrusts his pelvis forward once and shrugs.

There ya go, sir.

Good. Do it again.

What for?

I said I want ya to do it again. That was just one time. I want you to thrust, thrust, thrust. Like that. See? Thrust, thrust, thrust, and just keep on going just like that.

Ya know how old I am, don't ya?

Sir. The customer lowers his head and looks at the floor for a moment, then raises it back up. Sir, I need ya to do this for me. Do ya want me to buy your stool? Do ya?

Well, yeah, sure, but—

So then do this for me. Thrust, thrust, thrust. Come on now. Thrust, thrust, thrust. Ya see that? Ya see how I'm doing that now? Thrust, thrust, thrust. Come on. Do it. Thrust, thrust, thrust.

Okay then. The old man thrusts his hips forward three times in a row and then stops.

Keep going.

But, sir, I'm tired.

Keep going.

I'm an old man for god's sake.

Goddammit. Just thrust them. Just thrust them, ya hear?

The clerk feels a tingling sensation in his stomach. He knows the stakes are high with this one—and the fact that he has not the slightest clue what those stakes are makes him that much more terrified.

Snap, snap, snap go the customer's fingers every time the clerk thrusts his hips, like those of a deranged man directing a chorus line of dancers inside his own head to which only he is privy.

The old clerk thrusts faster and faster, but keeps having to stop in between to catch his breath.

Come on, come on, says the customer. Thrust, thrust. Thrust, thrust.

The old man's back finally gives as he totters forward, barely catching his balance on the stool.

I can't do this anymore, sir. I just can't.

Okay, okay. That's fine. That's perfect. Come on down now. Come on down.

The clerk steps down from the stool, hunched over, winded and wincing in pain. So, would ya like me to wrap it up for ya?

It's not the same.

Sir?

It's not the same. That stool isn't the same as that one there.

So, you're saying you don't want it then?

No, I still want it. It's not the same though, ya see? Do ya see that now? It's not the same as the other one, no sir.

The clerk has neither the courage nor energy to haggle. Sure, I see it. I see.

But I'm gunna take it home with me now and make it the same, okay?

Okay then. That's a good idea. I'll ring ya up.

I need some paint.

What's that?

Paint, paint. I need some paint. The customer with the crooked nose pounds his fist on the counter. Some paint, goddammit. To make it the same. It's not the same. I need to make it the same. Like yours. The same.

Alright then. Okay. Well. We got some cans of spray paint if—

Yessir. Spray paint would be nice. Spray paint should work just fine.

Alright then. Well, let me go in the back there again and see what I got, if ya just gimme a minute.

That's all I can give ya, I'm afraid.

The clerk swallows his breath hard as the customer's eyes lock on his own.

Right. Well, okay then, sir. Be back as quick as I can then.

The customer with the crooked nose looks up at the television once more. The giant man has vanished, his podium now empty in the background and barely visible behind the scrawling black tickertape.

A MID-AGED MAN surveys the city landscape outside the window of his new office. His eyes trace the sequence of skyscrapers and smokestacks, their tops cascading toward a meandering gray river dotted with ferries and cargo ships whose uppermost beams and pipes barely clear their way under the arches of the interborough bridge—a structural marvel whose concrete deck carries the vehicular tonnage of the morning rush hour, its reflection hovering over the water with a steely majesty. In the hazy distance, hardly noticeable to the naked eye, lie the faintest hints of the rolling green and brown mountaintops that separate the old world from the modern one, the rural from the metropolitan.

With one hand holding a phone to his ear and the other combing the graying tufts of his hair, his eyes return to what they fixate on most: the golden steeple of the old church directly across the street—the very same church he attends every Sunday morning. Even if this new job position of his does not pan out as planned, at least he will have the golden steeple outside his window.

And his family at home.

Yup. That's where I'm going, honey. Soon as I get off the phone with you, I'll be driving on up there. Should be pretty interesting. I mean, there's no way anyone lives there now—not a chance. I'm guessing it's just been sitting there abandoned for more than twenty years. Paperwork must have fallen through the cracks, that's all. Uh-huh. Well, given where it's located, it makes sense. Yup. They just want me to take some snapshots of what I see so they can show it to the foreclosure services contractor. But I'm wondering if there will even be anything left of the house when I get there—it's been so long, you know? Yup. I'll be sure to snap some extras for the road—I imagine it's gorgeous up there. Okay, you too, honey. See you at dinner. Give my little girl a kiss. Okay now. Love you. Bye.

HEY, TWINKIE—how am I supposed to go ahead and do this with ya makin so much of a goddamn racket there? says the man with the crooked nose standing on his shiny new step stool behind an ailing and broken-down horse, his trousers down to his ankles.

A dog—a straggly-haired mix of brown and white—wags its tail in the corner of the barn, just in the man's line of sight, whimpering and tilting its head this way and that.

Maybe ya wish I was doing this with you instead, eh?

The dog barks once, then growls.

Well, this here what I'm gunna do here has got nothin to do with you or what I feel about ya. Besides, I don't swing that way, ya hear? So, just go on and chase some squirrels or somethin, or maybe chase one of them birds who've been shittin on my porch like it was their very own to shit on. Go on and git now. Do somethin useful for a change instead of hangin around here and followin me wherever I go, watching me in whatever I do. Go on now and scram, ya hear?

The dog lowers itself to the floor of the barn, its front paws a pillow for its head, its tail still wagging in the back.

Fine then. Suit yourself. I'm gunna do what I'm gunna do whether you're here or not here. It's Gracie here I'm more concerned about. She's got more manners than I do. Me, I couldn't care less if the whole world was in this here barn watching me do this thing that I'm gunna do. Got nothin to hide, no sir. This thing here—it ain't a bad thing, ya hear? No, it ain't bad just cuz other folks would say it is. Who are people to judge in this world? Who are people to judge what is decent and what is not decent, what is good and what is not good? Ya think this thing that I do makes me not a good man? Ya think this is what's gunna make me go to hell? Well, I might go to hell, but it won't be for this—no, sir. This here what I'm doing—it ain't wrong, nor is it insane. Do ya think I'm insane? Do ya think I do what I do cuz I'm some sorta insane lunatic who can't control his urges? No, my friend. That ain't me. I ain't insane. Everything I do is well-thought-out, yessir. Everything I do is out of love, not wickedness. I love this horse. I once loved a woman, but she is no longer here now, is she? But sometimes, Twinks—and sorry if ya think this is crazy now—but sometimes I believe that my beloved Grace is still here, still with us, living inside this here horse inside this here barn. Ya may well think I'm crazy for thinking that—well, okay then. But this here horse—she don't think I'm crazy. No, sir. She sure don't. She knows she's a vessel for someone else now. Otherwise, if she weren't a vessel for my beloved, she'd might be just about dead right now, never mind deaf, would she not? Yessir, she would. Cuz love—that's what keeps it all going on, ya hear? If you don't have love, if you don't get love, if you don't give love—well, what's the point of livin is what I'm sayin here.

So, I love ya, Twinks, and, yes, I know ya love me too, but this here love between me and this horse right here—well, it's just a different kind of love for reasons beyond you or me. So, I can understand if you're feelin sort of left out and full of envy there in your little corner there, but this here is somethin I gotta do. It's the only way—and I don't give two shits if you believe me or don't believe me, approve or disapprove—but it's the only way that I can keep my beloved alive on this here earth. Through this act only—understand? So, if you have any problem with that—well, ya know where the exit is, my friend. Just remember to shut the door behind ya, okay? I don't wanna have to be thinkin about catchin no draft here while I'm in the middle of doing what I'm doing. Either way though, thanks for listenin, Twinks. You've always been a listener's listener—I'll give ya that, yessir.

Alright then. Where was I?

IT WAS IN THE MORNING that he first felt it, when he looked out the window of his office. The steel arches of the bridges, the ripples in the water made by the boats, the billowing smokestacks, the flickering radio towers of the skyscrapers, the far-off misty mountaintops.

And, of course, the golden steeple of the church.

An epiphany? Is that what it was? Is that what he was feeling when he chatted with his wife on the phone about his day's assignment? That a higher meaning was waiting for him out there in the wilderness, away from the modern confines of city life, amidst all the green foliage and the sweet smell of tilled soil in the air?

The air, the fresh mountain air—the idea excites him, arouses him even.

Spiritually, of course. And existentially.

Sexually? Perhaps that as well.

Driving on the winding roads of the backwoods, he feels a certain kind of giddiness, but it is a controlled giddiness. He hums along with the melodies coming from the radio, but never does he sing along. Epiphany or no epiphany, he is on the job. He has to keep himself maintained at all times.

He imagines making love to his wife in the tall grass. It is not something he has ever done or sees himself ever really doing, but he cannot help himself from imagining it.

How grand it would be. Naked in the grass. Skin against skin. On mother nature's bed.

Make a boy, a voice inside him whispers. Make a boy.

The words come muttering out of his mouth as his silver sedan pulls onto the crunch of the gravel driveway of the residence he has come to see.

The farmhouse—it is still there. It looks like it has suffered some weather damage—the window shutters askew, paint peeling off of every-where, branches and leaves covering the roof and chimney, the screen door in front hanging off its hinge—but otherwise it looks to be in working condition, albeit neglected-looking and desolate.

He snaps a dozen or so photos at various angles, and then walks up onto the porch.

He does not bother to knock on the door—he just lets himself in. No one in their right mind would be living in this titanic mess. Books and bottles on the floor everywhere. He thinks he sees some fresh wet spots near where the bottles lie, but then surmises it is just rainwater that has leaked in from some tiny hole in the wall or ceiling.

Or maybe it is from some campers trashing the place—there is always that. In fact, it must have been that. He can still smell the ash from the fireplace.

Those campers must have been here quite recently. Very recently—he can smell tobacco smoke, too.

Or maybe that's marijuana?

Who knows?

And who cares anyway?

He enters the kitchen. Plates caked with the residue of dried-up food are stacked up high in the sink. The refrigerator sounds like it is on, but when he opens it, the light is off, and so is the air. He sees cola cans and beer bottles and an unopened loaf of bread inside. But the milk carton—its expiration date is past due, but only by a week.

Yep, someone must've been trespassing in here recently, for sure.

The whole kitchen smells of mold. He feels a queasiness in the pit of his stomach. He exits the room and heads up the staircase.

He sees three bedrooms upstairs—two that are empty, and one with a single bed in it. The one with the bed in it still has the box spring sheet on it. It has a large stain in the middle.

Well, someone was having fun in here, he mutters.

He thinks about his wife for a moment, and about the tall grass again, but then he sees the clock on the old nightstand next to the bed. Its hands are in the right places. There is no cord running behind it—it is running on batteries. Fresh batteries.

Someone is living here, he thinks. Something about it all makes him suddenly feel unsafe. He exits the bedroom, walks back down the stairs, and marches straight out the front door, one hand holding on tight to his clipboard, the other fumbling to shove a pen into the pocket of his slacks.

He is about to open his car door when he hears some noise over his shoulder—some clanking and some grunting. The sounds are coming from the red barn that stands a good couple dozen or so yards next to the farmhouse.

Does this farm still have livestock on it? He has to see this for himself. He is afraid to go look, but he is too curious. Moreover, it is his job to go look. The farmhouse, the barn, the land—it is all now the property of his employer, and he, as an employee representative, has a right to be on it as much as anyone else.

But who or what else is on there with him on that property?

He must find out. This is a test, he thinks. My first test at my new job position, yes, but also a much grander test.

The feeling—the one he felt driving in the woods—comes rushing back to him. Yes, this is it. This is the moment. This is the revelation he had been waiting for.

He suddenly feels at ease. He imagines what will be in that barn will change his life somehow. For the better. And didn't his wife want pictures—isn't that what she had wanted? Well, an abandoned barn filled with cows, pigs or whatever—oh, that would be something, wouldn't it? One with nature—this is what they meant by it, yes?

The words rushed through his head again: Make that boy. Make that boy. Make that boy. Yes, in some weird and mysterious way—whatever was in store from him around the corner—this was all going to make him earn it.

The clanking had already stopped. Just a faint grunt now and then.

When he peeks through the door, the first thing that grabs his attention are the rafters, their beams intersecting like giant crosses.

He thinks of the church outside his office window, the steeple. It is as if it had followed him here, he thinks.

God is with him in this barn, yes.

Oh, God.

Who said that? Was that his own voice? Or was it an angel's voice inside his own head?

Oh, Grace.

It is not an angel's voice, he thinks to himself. It is His.

He sees the horse and the shadowy figure behind the horse, but the intersecting beams obstruct what would otherwise be a clear view, so he walks slowly and carefully toward the stall to get a better look.

Oh, God.

Oh, Grace.

Oh, God.

Oh, Grace.

The voice. So baritone. So reverberating. It is rhythmic. Hypnotic even.

Grace.

Gracie.

Grace.

Gracie.

Gracie? The word slips out from the visitor's mouth.

By the time the startled man with the crooked nose pulls himself out from behind the horse, it is too late for the Jesus-loving foreclosure specialist to escape the sprinkle of the man's holy fluid from raining on top of his head.

Instead the specialist stands there wetted and in shock at the revelation the Lord, our Father, has beset upon him.

After staring at the man on the stool for a moment or so, the specialist-turned-intruder turns in horror and makes a dash for it.

Hey, you son bitch. Get back here. The short man with the long and crooked nose pulls up his trousers and jumps down from his stool, and begins to run after the intruder. As his trousers slip back down to his thighs, then his knees, he flails his fists down hard on the hood of the frightened and horrified urban dweller's sedan as it speeds off the gravel driveway and back up the winding road from which it came.

Yeah, ya better run, motherfucker.

The foreclosure specialist rolls up his windows and looks at himself in the rearview mirror, the top of his gray tufts caked in a holy glop of human-made hair gel.

He thinks about the man, the horse. The barn, the house. The church, the steeple. His wife and the high grass. The air. That magnificent, fresh mountain air he no longer trusted.

He keeps his car windows rolled up for the entire drive back into the city.

He takes deep breath after deep breath, convincing himself that his belief in God, though now tested, will never shatter.

The golden steeple. The church. Perhaps he will worship there more often, he thinks to himself.

And let's not forget: he still had his family—his wife, his little girl.

Just about the time he crosses the bridge into the city of his vocation and residence, a low voice rises from the depths of his own muddled mind.

Make that boy, the voice says. Make that boy. Just make that boy and you will find the Lord Jesus Christ once again.

When his car phone rings, he screams in terror, stamping his foot on the brake, the car screeching across the avenue, out toward the crowded intersection.

CAN YA keep a secret? This is off the record what I'm about to tell ya. It would be embarrassing for me and my family if this, what I'm about to tell ya, got out in any way. I don't even know why I'm going to tell ya what I'm about to tell ya, but since it sounds like ya did your homework on everything else about me and my family, why the hell wouldn't I tell ya what I'm about to tell ya? Besides, I kind of like ya. Ya remind me of my guidance counselor from back in high school. He helped me through some rough times, and I remember I could tell him anything, and he never judged, but I never told him this one thing I'm about to tell ya.

Look, as you already now, me and him—our friend in question, I mean, not the guidance counselor—go way back to when we were kids. My family used to own the farm down the road from where his family was, and our families—we had known each other a long time, yessir. Ya might even say we were close for a while, me and him. But my family—we sold the farm before things got out of hand. Lost a few on the sale, but at least it wasn't like his family's situation. Well, in any event, there was this one time, before we was even teenagers, he told me to meet him in the stalls—ya know, the horse stalls, where his family kept dem horses in? So, I went in there to where dem stalls were, but I couldn't see him anywhere. I called out his name a few times. Some people called him Junior, but I never called him by that name, no sir. I only called him by his real name. I don't think he liked that other name. Junior, I mean. He never said so, but I could tell he never liked being called that name. Probably made him feel like he was less than, if ya know what I mean. So, there I was, calling his name out, calling his name out—no answer. So, what I did was I just turned myself around and walked back out from where I came from. I saw him the next day in school, and I said to him where were ya, and he said in the stalls. And I said, well, I was calling your name out—how come ya didn't answer? He said, well, I couldn't on account of what I was doing in there, and I said what was it was you doing in there, and he said come back same time tomorrow and you'll see just what. I told him, well, ya better be there then cuz I won't be coming back again otherwise.

So, same time next day, I go back to dem stalls again. I call out his name again. His real name. But, once again, I get no answer. I call one more time, two more times—no answer. I decide the hell with him and start walking myself back out again. Figured it was some sort of prank where he's got me calling out like an idiot, so I figured fuck him, I'm outta here. But then I heard somethin. Wasn't sure if it was one of dem horses that made the noise, but it definitely didn't sound human. Sounded a lot like a gruntin, a snortin, or what not. So, I said, Junior, Junior, is that you, Junior, not that I ever thought it was him or nothin. Figured maybe some pig got loose. Junior, Junior, I say again. That's when I feel a tap on my shoulder, and it's him, all pissed off and such. He also looked a bit stoned. I said why you so pissed at me when I'm the one calling out to ya like an idiot just like I did two days before? And he said, well, I don't like being called Junior. And I said I know, I know, sorry bout that, but ya got me all worked up on account of your not answering me again. He said listen, I gotta tell ya something. He said I never shared this with anyone else, but I'm gunna share it with you. He said ya gotta promise me ya won't tell anyone else about it. So, I said okay then, I won't, but what was it? He says do ya wanna get high with me, and I say sure, and I had no problem saying sure to him cuz I had gotten high with him a few times before that time. One of our neighbors on one of dem ranches near us had a cousin who was a part-time mule. Drug mule, that is. Well, in any event, I tell him yeah, sure, I'll get high with ya, so he says come here then, I want ya to try somethin. So, I followed him into one of dem stalls where one of dem horses was. He tells me to stand right behind the horse. I looked at him like he was crazy—I didn't want to get kicked in the head or nothin, but he told me not to worry, she's a friendly horse. He had one of them big yella page books of his on the ground behind the horse, and he wanted me to stand on it, so I stood on it even though I felt uneasy about it. But he kind of had this way about him. And he never had steered me wrong before, especially when it came to gettin high, so I trusted him. And aside from drugs, we had also experimented with other things together, if ya know what I mean. Ya know, the silly-innocent-touchy kind of stuff—the kind of stuff all kids do when they're just being kids.

But that's neither here nor there.

Well, anyway, gettin back to what I was sayin: he took the horse by the tail. What I mean is that he lifted it up, and pointed to where her you-know-what was. Ya see that? he says to me. I just cleaned her. They say if ya toss a horse's salad long enough ya get a buzz.

Toss a what? I says to him. I had never heard that before then—toss a salad. I had no idea what that meant back then. It wasn't until many years later when I—well, I mean, when I heard it again—that I ever looked up on it. But look, like I said, I went through some rough times back then. My mama was dead, my pa was beatin me up real good whenever he could, so no one had to convince me about wanting to get high. I was what they now call vulnerable, but I don't even think anyone used that sort of word back then—vulnerable. So, there I was all vulnerable and such and wanting to get high, and he said, Go on now—lick it. And I looked at him like he was stark goddamn crazy, but he didn't blink, ya know? He had one of them faces you could trust. I know that's hard to believe now, but it's true. I mean, what did I know? Who ever heard of tossing a horse's salad before, never mind anyone else's salad, when you were as many years young as I was back then? So, what I decided—in my head, I mean—was that I would lick just a tiny wee bit in there, ya know? Just kind of go quick in and go quick out. So, I stick my tongue out and bring my head toward the, ya know, the hole there. I remember thinkin at least it looked clean like he said it was gunna be, so I kept on moving my head closer to it, closer and closer until my tongue finally hit what I thought was it. And I gotta tell ya, while it didn't taste like much, it did taste clean like he said it was gunna be. So, then he went and whispered in my ear to really get in there and lick around a bit, so that's what I did. I mean, back then, I probably would have tried anything if it meant me gettin high and not having to think about my sorry excuse for a life. I mean, I found God later, but back then, God was just a word to me.

Well, in any event, as I'm sure you can guess, it didn't take long before I realized I was being played. Went in there thinkin I was gunna get myself high tossing a horse's salad, and all I ended up with was a dirty sanchez right on the kisser. Needless to say, I nearly barfed my own tongue out, it was so awful.

He said, That's what ya get for calling me Junior.

The good thing about that whole thing was that at least for a good while it made me forget about all my problems. But believe me, those problems of mine all came back just as about as quick as they went away.

Yep. A dirty sanchez. Help yourself to lookin that one up as well, yessir.

But more than anything, even more than that prank, was the look he gave me after it happened. He wasn't laughing or nothin. He didn't even look stoned anymore. Just looked real serious. I wouldn't say mean—he didn't look mean, really—just serious.

Well, hey—like I said, this is one that's off the record. I mean, I just felt it would give ya some insight into what kind of guy he was back then. Me, like I said, I don't think I would've done what I did if it weren't for my situation—a situation I'm sure you're aware of if you've done your homework and such, which it seems you already did. It was my old man's fault, really—that's why I did what I did with that poor horse, that's why I was the way I was, and that's why I forgive myself. Daddy and mommy issues is what I had, and—ya know what?—that's okay, is what I say. Cuz I'm comfortable with who I am now. And I can say that now, now that I have God's grace in my life.

Yep. Right in the nick of time, I found Him, amen.

What is it they say? Whatever doesn't kill ya makes ya—what is it?—more strong, right? But, ya know, let's still keep this all off the record regardless—for my family's sake, I mean. No reason for the missus and the kids to know such things about the man they know and love. Heaven knows they've already suffered enough from my tenuous relations with our friend in question.

Very tenuous, that is.

HOLD STILL, Junior. Hold still, goddammit.
    Good boy.

He wakes up and can no longer see.

Too much whiskey, is his first thought.

He is not sure if that is a proven medical fact—that an excessive intake of whiskey can lead to blindness—but that is the first thought that runs through his hung-over head the moment he wakes up.

A blind man with a deaf horse—the utter cruelty.

He can hear his beloved mare whinnying in the corner of the stall. Based on the trajectory of the sound, he can tell she is lying on her side most likely, but is now beginning to rise off the barn floor.

Gracie. My dear, Gracie. What has become of me?

The words—Grace, Gracie, Grace, Gracie—they are no longer swimming in his head, but instead being screamed out of his mouth in primal terror.

The darkness, the stifling and impenetrable darkness.

I won't survive it, he thinks. Better yet: I will not allow myself to survive it.

He feels around the barn—he knows it well enough that he can see the whole layout of it in his head. It has been his home within a home for so many months now—even years, really. He feels around for something sharp or something that could be made into something sharp. A knife. An empty bottle. Something he can break off and bury into his neck. It would be a painful way to die, but with his life having been pain on top of pain, loss on top of loss, it would be the only fitting way to die.

With pain.

But the brief pain of slitting his throat open—and he sincerely believes it would be quite brief, the pain from this endeavor, for would not his oxygen-deprived brain expire before the rest of him did?—would be better than the grueling pain of complete and infinite darkness for years on end, of being able to see nothing but his memories, his losses, the things he squandered, of Grace, of Grace, of Grace.

His hands scampering everywhere for the right object, he becomes infatuated with the idea of terminating his own self. Why had he not done this long ago? Why struggle with the hurt and anguish when he can put a quick end to it all? Why is there a need to float around in this world when there is no one who loves him to watch him float? No one needs him. No woman. No man. No child. Nor was he in need. There is no longer anything for him to need or want. He wants nothing of this world and the world wants nothing of him—that has been clear for some time now.

He hears the sound of laughter. It takes him several seconds to realize it is his own.

He has finally found what will bring him joy: relief from pain.

He feels muscles in his face that he has not used in years. Is he smiling? Is this what smiling feels like? He cannot remember.

His hand touches something hard and sharp. It hooks around his thumb and dangles in the air. He feels it with his other hand: shears. Shears he had used for clipping—

The first kick throws him about a half dozen feet or so, and the next kick right after that sends the shears flying out of his hand and his head crashing into the barn door.

Yes, the barn door—he can tell it is the barn door by the creaking sound it makes as it is flung open.

His head throbs from the impact—he can feel it swelling as he lies face down on the ground outside the barn.

He rolls over on his back. Something drips from his eyes.

Must be blood, he thinks.

He wipes away at his eyes, then considers the futility of such an act as he now can no longer see anything anyhow. But as he wipes and wipes, he begins to see a faint glimmer of light in the corner of his eye.

The aftershock of blindness, he thinks to himself. An inner light short-circuiting inside his brain.

His fingers pick away at the viscous fluid oozing from his eyes and the light grows broader and more penetrating.

He stops his fingers for a moment to consider this new development. Is whiteness better than darkness? No, it is not. It is still nothingness nonetheless.

He claws away again at the sticky mass around his eyes with furious energy. He is eager to get back to the barn to finish the deed.

He gets up from the ground again, but as he rises something kicks him in the back again.

Goddamn you, Gracie.

He lies there for a moment, then turns over on his back again. He looks up at where he knows the sky is and the first thing he sees is the moon.

His mare has kicked him into seeing the world again.

Or was that his beloved Grace in there that had done the kicking?

The throbbing pain in his head and back from the blows administered is excruciating. He holds his hands to his head, then holds them out in front of his face.

They look like brown gloves.

He wipes away at his eyes again and examines his fingers in the moonlight.

Manure. That was all it was. That was all it ever was when it came to him and his life: fucking manure.

He lumbers back into the barn and sees the mare, standing, as always, in the shit of her own making, her stall long overdue for a cleaning.

After clearing out the rest of the manure from his eyes, he grabs a shovel, enters the mare's stall, and begins to dig.

OH, HOW HE GLOWS even now in the pitch-black of the bedroom, observes the brown woman with the chiseled cheekbones. A giant man with a craterless moon for a head and only evil in his heart. How could I have ended up being so wrong about him? What turned his heart so cold? How can anyone sleep with such monstrous thoughts and horrible deeds weighing over his conscience?

Conscience? He has no conscience. No room for that when it comes to this hateful man.

She could leave him. She could walk out of this room, awaken the boy, and the two of them, they could leave. She could tell the guards that they're just going to see her mother—she is feeling ill and would like to see her grandson, she would say.

But the guards will know. He's trained them all to think like him. He's gotten into all their heads already, never mind this whole city. They won't let her get away with it. They'll bring her right back to him.

Like gravity, says a voice inside the woman's head. Like a moon with gravity, this man who lies next to me is.

She studies the sleeping giant next to her in the bed, her face hovering over his own.

So very luminous and tranquil in the night, he is. Always sleeping so perfectly still on his back. How she would love to disrupt his spiteful serenity, to put an end to it all. If only there was a pillow large enough for that gigantic head of his.

If only she had the strength, the will.

NEITHER ONE of them knows she is referred to, in human language, as a horse, as they, salivating from a grassy hilltop sparsely populated by trees, watch her graze back and forth across the pasture that spreads for acres in front of a dilapidated farmhouse at the end of a winding, dusty road. They are neither concerned with the nomenclature assigned to their prey, nor aware of the grieving man with the crooked nose living inside the farmhouse. They are only concerned with sating their never-ending appetite for raw animal flesh.

The pair of wolves, having agreed to make a meal out of the horse on the pasture, cock their heads up toward the full moon and shriek their staccato howls, not stopping even after a half-dozen are so of their brethren gather with them, joining voices with their own in the moonlit ecstasy on the crest of the hill.

The horse continues to graze uninterrupted in the center of the pasture, unaware of the boisterous frenzy on top of the hill incited by her presence. She is too far away from the wolves to hear their wild and hungry sounds, as she is all but deaf, the consequence of a previous nocturnal ambush executed by a predator of diminutive size.

Almost as soon as a few more members of the pack join the chorus on top of the hill, their snarls and wails come to a close. The largest of their kin, a lean and muscular giant with a handsome black coat of fur, his white muzzle speckle-stained with blood, has arrived to lead them down the slick slope of the hill, still moist from the midday rain.

The horse does not hear them trudging down the slope, but as four of them move a few yards onto the pasture, her nostrils pick up the vague scent of the perspiration and filth covering their furry bodies and the foul smell of their digestive fluids dripping from their open mouths. When she looks up, she sees only one of them, her vision now having also gone awry from the venom injected by her previous attacker, but dismisses the canine creature as simply a stray dog from one of the neighboring ranches, a common encounter that never comes to anything.

She puts her head back down in the grass and eats.

The giant wolf continues to lead his army of hunters down the slippery slope of the hill, then drops behind them to lead from the back like a seasoned general waiting to see his strategy executed. He knows his smallest warriors are less likely to be detected by their target, so he always, at the appropriate moment of their murderous ritual, sends them to the front lines, letting them be the ones to make the kill, to drag the carcass to his feet in order to allow him that inaugural bite. His days of doing the heavy labor, though ingrained in his memory, are, as far as he is concerned, well behind him. He is the king now, and the king wins all the spoils, does he not? He is content in letting his pack of killers do all the killing, save for the few occasions when his physical exertions are necessary for the mission's success and his superior strength and tactical skills are the difference between feast and famine.

This occasion, he thinks, as he licks his front fangs over and over in an unconscious rhythm and watches his pack edge their way closer to its prey, is not one of those occasions. There is nothing about this occasion that leads him to believe that this night's offensive will be any different from most of the preceding ones—that is, quick and easy—especially given that the prey in question still seems to be unaware of the pack's presence on the pasture. What a reward for such an expeditious takedown this would be, for this night's prey was larger and meatier than those on most nights.

The bigger, the tastier, he thinks to himself.

The horse sees a shadow on the ground only a few feet or so from where her mouth chews at the wet grass. She looks up expecting to see her owner or perhaps the stray dog that has trespassed on his property, but that is not what she sees.

The first wolf growls and grits its teeth when the brown mare locks eyes with him. Then more growling comes from the horse's other side, as two more wolves, slightly larger than the first, gnash their teeth at her.

A tear drips from the horse's eye, as her heart beats harder and faster. She is about to gallop back to the barn when four more snarling wolves crouch their legs low to the ground and block her path. She prances around this way and that, but the wolves hold their ground. The pack has her surrounded in a circle formation. She thinks about running straight through one of the wolves—perhaps she can outrun them all—but with a circle of reinforcements waiting right behind them that is not a viable option.

The wolves creep in closer and closer until there is no room for her to pace in either direction. Their bloodstained general remains in the distance, watching, waiting, licking his chops as his strategy unfolds. He belts out a howl so guttural that it wakes the birds from the trees behind him, sending them flying from their perch, and makes the horse shudder as her legs give out from under her. She closes her eyes, hoping that the wolves would vanish, that the dire situation she finds herself in is just a terrifying nightmare, but when she reopens them, the wolves, though confounded for a moment, remain in their positions, their yellow eyes dilated and glowing in the dark, ready to pounce.

The mare continues to lie on her side, spinning her long legs in a circle to keep the wolves at bay. One strike from her hoof, the wolves know, could be fatal. Around in circles on the ground she goes, the yellow eyes of the wolves glowing like fireflies in the night. Every few seconds or so, one of the wolves lunges forward, but for every lunge she answers with a kick, backing the aggressor away, leaving him barking in violent frustration. It goes on like this for a minute or so—the spinning, the lunging, the kicking—until one of the wolves manages to seize the mare from the back of the neck, causing her to flip over and whinny in excruciating agony. This flipping over crushes the wolf that has her in his fanged grip, but also creates an opening for the others to come in and pounce on her belly as she lands on her back.

The giant wolf at the foot of the hill moves in closer. The plan is working, making him crave the night's prey even more. He belts out another hungry howl that reverberates for miles, through the trees, toward the mountains hidden behind them.

The wolves go to work on her underside—her ribs, her belly, her womanhood—the mare shrieking in terror, her condition soon giving way to a trauma-induced silence.

The mare feels small hunks of her body being torn off, but the pain fades into the background. Her eyes are so filled with tears, she can no longer see. Her ears hear nothing as they are tugged and mutilated. She no longer feels her legs kicking, but indeed they are, and that is the only thing keeping her alive.

Her blood-curdling whinnying also keeps her alive, for they hurt the ears of the attacking wolves at times, causing them to turn away at the high-pitched sound, before lunging back to finish up the kill.

Her loud whinnying also jostles her owner out of his drunken slumber. He had dozed off, as he often did, in his decades-old recliner in the family room of the farmhouse, an empty flask of whiskey in his lap. He hears the screeching cries coming from outside and suddenly remembers having left his beloved mare out in the pasture, a consequence of his recurring negligence.

He grabs a shotgun hanging above the mantel, never minding the piercing pain inside his head, for it is a pain that has already made its home inside there during most hours of the day.

As he barrels onto the porch, he can hear the wolves—yes, he knows they can only be wolves—growling and yodeling in their ravenous ecstasy far out in the pasture. He fires out three quick shots in the air and hears the sounds of creatures scurrying for cover.

He hops the wooden fence and runs toward the sound of the commotion, the moonlight picking up more and more of what he is headed toward as he runs. A couple dozen yards or so into the pasture, he feels the warm squish of horse manure on his bare feet, but that does not break his pace.

He fires two more shots, careful not to waste more than might be necessary if the going were to get rough.

Please let that be enough to make them go away, a voice inside his head says. Please let that be enough.

It is the trembling voice of a fearful child.

By the time he reaches his wounded mare, only two wolves remain—the same two, unbeknownst to him, whose shadows were first cast on his precious horse. They back away from their prized prey, but then stand their ground as the man with the glistening shotgun in his hands aims the tip of its barrel back and forth, in staccato fashion, from one to the other. He quickly makes up his mind to shoot one of them before they spread themselves far enough apart from one another that it would be hard to keep an eye on them both, then fires away. The bullet grazes the target on the side of the cheek—or perhaps it is just the fur of the cheek, for it is too dark for him to be certain—and the wolf runs for cover back up the hill. By the time he swings his barrel toward his next intended target, it has already run as well.

The man with the crooked nose takes a deep breath, hunches over, vomits on his own shit-stained feet, and then stands up straight again. For a moment, he thinks he hears something sifting through the taller clusters of grass, but it is all clear.

He looks down at his beloved mare.

The slick grooves and gushing gashes across her body glisten like red oil in the moonlight, as she lies motionless on her side, her belly bleeding out all around her in a cesspool of her own fluids.

For a moment, the man with the crooked nose is reminded of the woman he loved and her last days—the quiet bloodletting from beneath her hospital gown.

Grace.

Gracie.

When his hand touches the side of her neck, the mare flinches violently and sits halfway up. Her state of shock so deep, it takes her a while to distinguish between the man kneeling before her and the wolves who had just attacked her.

It's okay, Gracie, says the man with the crooked nose. It's just me now. No one else but me.

Her eyes look glossy to him. It is her eyes more than her flesh wounds that make her almost unrecognizable. Her eyes speak to him: they say that things will never be the same again, that the demons had gotten to her, to him, to this rundown wreck of a farm they call home.

He spots something on the ground nearby—something raw-looking, a chunk of torn-off flesh perhaps. He starts to walk toward this object, thinking it best to pick up the pieces of his horse that are on the pasture so no more predators would come sniffing by. He would hose down the rest of the bloodbath the next morning—maybe just throw a tarp on it for now.

Did he even own a tarp? He cannot remember. His body aches too much to even think.

He looks at his mare again. He knows she needs medical attention right away. He begins to kneel down close to her again when something suddenly hits him like a truck across his back, knocking him forward. It steps on the back of his head and makes a deep grunting sound, deeper than any grunt from anything with four legs that he has ever heard. When he looks up, for a moment or two he swears it is a small black horse with a white muzzle and canine incisors, but when it jumps onto the mare's back and sinks its fangs into her body, no one needs to tell him what it really is.

The man with the crooked nose watches helplessly as the giant wolf jerks its head backward and rips out a hunk of flesh from the mare's back, shaking the gigantic morsel at the moonlit sky.

The mare kicks her front legs up in the air as the pain shoots up her spine, knocking the predator off her, causing it to fall on its back and roll several yards. As the giant wolf shakes off the hard fall, the man with the crooked nose grabs his shotgun from the ground, and aims the tip of its barrel at the great beast.

It is larger than any wolf he has ever seen.

The giant wolf snarls, gnashing its jagged teeth at the man holding the shotgun. It takes a step forward, testing the shooter in front of him, then another.

The shooter has his doubts. He knows he is not a good shot—not in his current condition—even with a target so close and so large. He takes a step back, fearing being too close to it would obscure it. The wolf sees this maneuver, taking it as a sign of weakness, and lunges at the shooter, who aims his shotgun, arches his back, and fires away in desperation at the target flying in his direction.

The whole world seems to screech around the man with the crooked nose as the giant wolf cries out and hits the ground. He could have sworn he saw something fly off the beast before it had landed in the tall grass, but just as quickly as it recovers its breath, the wolf darts off up the hill, toward the dark and twisted trees that make up what people refer to as the woods, or, in perhaps more formal human nomenclature, the forest.

SOMETIMES HE has dreams about them.

In these dreams, he sits on his porch, watching the sun rise or set, and then out from the hills, like a platoon of soldiers, they come marching down, their briefcases in one hand, their clipboards in the other, their ties swinging from side to side across their chests, their sleeves half-rolled up, some with hair on their heads, some without, all of them much taller than he.

Some of them smile, some of them look like all business, some of them snarl aloud with blood dripping out of their mouths.

They all wear spectacles.

One carries a giant wooden sign with the letter F spray-painted in red.

There he is, one of them says.

Let's fuck her first, says another.

And then the man with the crooked nose runs to the barn and tells his beloved mare to go, to run, to flee, to never come back, for it is not safe here anymore, it is not safe, but she who is not capable of hearing stays put where she is, showing no signs of alarm or terror, as she rolls onto her back and waits as they all stuff their way into her tiny stall, some jumping the walls on either side, some of their faces turning into the faces of gray wolves, their teeth transforming into fangs, their gums soaked with blood and foam, the yellow of their eyes flickering on and off in the dimly lit barn as they chew and push their way into her, until he holds out his pistol and shoots at anything that moves, the bullets landing everywhere but on the wild men with their lupine heads, but enough to scare them back into the hills, each and every one of them, except the one who mounts the F sign on the lawn in front of his house and the few others nailing up the boards into the front door and windows. And then the footsteps, the quiet footsteps behind him, him spinning to see who it is—another lupine head in a suit?—no, but it is Grace, his Grace, his beloved Grace, her hair slicked back behind her ears, her eyes dilating in the moonlight, her body covered in blood and semen and mud, the bones of her elbows torn out through her skin, her breasts dangling in chewed-up strings of flesh, the head of their half-made child swinging back and forth against the ground, its feet caught in the ripped-out hole of her womb.

His heart no longer beating inside his chest, he runs for his life across the pasture, toward the dark woods, the red moon pulsating low above the ground, its rhythm shaking the earth beneath his feet, until he falls down, then rises up, and awakens into the reality of his own drunken and chilly nakedness, his moist and feverish body curled up at the knees in a shaking heap of pasty white flesh, soiled and foul.

---∘)∘C∕∾∘(∘---

SOMETHING IN the great wolf's head does not feel right, a nausea that grows heavier and heavier, as he shoulders his way deeper and deeper into the forest. He feels the stinging rawness from the absent claw with every step as the gastric juices in his stomach and chest overwork themselves. Perhaps this is all a byproduct of an appetite gone unsatisfied mixed with the adrenaline of a gunshot wound. But his head—that is what concerns him the most as he trots and leaps over wet stone and fallen branch, making his way home to the cave where his family holds shelter. It feels like something has spread itself around his skull, clamped itself down on him like a vise, a tarry syrup oozing its way through his vessels.

Objects he sees—trees, bushes, boulders, bullfrogs, salamanders, squirrels—seem to flow into one another, losing their physical outline. He sees things only in colors, then in shape again, then colors, then shape. His body temperature fluctuates in violent shifts, causing him to shiver with the chills at one moment, then burst into hot sweats the next.

His head is too heavy to allow him to gaze up at the sky—he tries it just once, and sees the moon spilling itself yellow over the trees above him.

A frantic ravenousness alternates with a burning need to defecate, and as he walks, he can feel a leaking warmth dripping down the back of his hind legs.

All this anatomical tumult, however, does not disrupt his pace. Fear and desperation only serve to push him further. It is only when he reaches a brook that he finally takes a breather. His memory in flux, he is not certain if it is a brook he has seen before on prior treks or if this is a new one created by the afternoon rain.

He has to drink—that he is certain of. He lowers his bloodstained muzzle into the water, but as he opens his mouth to lick, something surges up inside of him and bursts out of his mouth in a fleshy clump of blood and phlegm. He watches the clump get whisked away by the slow-moving flow of the brook. As he follows it in bewildered terror—his raging ailment no longer a figment of his imagination—he catches a glimpse of something a few yards down the bank.

A body. A body stretched out on its side, its fur damp with mud, its eyes swollen shut, its muzzle inches away from the streaming water, its nostrils infested with flies and red ants, its tongue drooping and hanging over the side of its half-open mouth, a congealing hole of stringy red and green.

It is a body he is familiar with, one that had once moved with an eager and confident stealth under his command.

He spots another one of his fallen comrades across the brook, belly down in the dirt, mosquitoes, basking in the moonlight, circling around its pointy ears, a bird—a sparrow, perhaps—picking around its eye sockets, swallowing whatever pieces of matter that can be pried from them.

The great wolf sees all this and heaves more of his own bile into the water.

In disgust.

In remorse.

In fear.

His thirst recedes, replaced by an urgency to bathe, to cool off. He takes a step into the brook. It is slow enough and shallow enough for him to cleanse himself. Wet and chilly from the water, he no longer feels the oozing heaviness around his head, and the gastric tumult of his body, while not entirely gone, has faded into the background, his injured paw more numb now than raw. His senses, if acute before the incident on the pasture, are now beyond alert.

He trudges on through the woods.

He decides to make the best out of what he has seen of his fallen comrades: He is stronger than they are. He made it past the brook, and they had not. His fever had broken, while theirs had gotten the better of them. Their deaths would only make the pack stronger.

An even stronger leader of an even stronger pack—that is what he has become. His wound would be a mark of valor, not vulnerability.

As these euphoric thoughts swim their circles around his brain, the great beast moves faster and faster through the forest, imagining his return home, eager to show off his latest battle scar to his kin.

He is almost home when he sees two more of his comrades—one on the ground on its side, the other on its back—overcome by whatever germ or virus was living in the meat of their latest prey.

Weak. They are weak, he thinks to himself. Rather than the remorse he felt earlier for his two other fallen comrades, this time he feels more anger—betrayal, even. Two down is one thing, but four? The latter two were among the largest of the pack. The largest and the strongest.

He gnashes his teeth down hard into his tongue. Perhaps the pack would have to hunt for smaller game until some of the younger members of the clan matured. But, with their fathers having perished, who will take the time to teach them to hunt, to fight, to share the spoils?

Anger soon gives way to hunger again. Hunger and thirst. The euphoric burst of adrenaline had already receded and the heavy nausea in his head and body had returned.

He hears the sound of rushing water up ahead of him, just past the next series of conifers. When he reaches the rushing brook—a brook much faster and deeper, and much more familiar, than the previous one he had encountered—he stops to drink, just enough to hold him for the last push toward home. He drinks with a forced vigor in spite of his deep exhaustion, but instead of the refreshing surge of energy he had hoped to experience again, he only feels much of the same of what was ailing him before he drank, only with more intensity. The melting visions return, and now something whistles and aches inside his ears, blocking out the sounds made by the creatures around him as they awaken with the first hints of sunlight. He thinks he hears something heavy traipsing several yards ahead of him—one of his surviving comrades perhaps?—but cannot tell if it is just whatever it is clogging up the inside of his ears playing a trick on him.

His fever grows and grows, his nostrils oozing red and green. The fluid clogging the inside of his ears has hardened, turning the world around him to silence. Every now and then, his body grazes off a tree, its rough bark cutting through his deep, black coat, scraping his skin. Not being able to distinguish between object and shadow, he collides right into the base of a tree, breaking the bones of his muzzle and jaw down the middle. He can no longer feel his tongue, just a numbing thickness.

He is certain that one of his toes—the one that had lost its claw perhaps?—has fallen off all together.

But he trudges on. His ailments and deformities would only make his legend grow. They all had to see. His family, his pack, the other elders. They all had to see him make it to the end.

When he reaches home, he sees the surviving members of his pack thrashing, gnashing and tugging at something among themselves—a hare perhaps. They had a rabid aura about them, one rooted, most likely, in whatever was infecting their insides. He wants to join them—he is starving, his stomach acids having burrowed a hole in his center—but his family must come first. He has to see them first so that they could witness him, his wounds, his valor, his against-all-odds survival. It is he who survived being shot—no one else.

Inside the cave, a cool air chills his hot and bloodied face. It is an air that is very familiar, but one that, on this occasion, also feels desolate and unused. He calls out to the darkness in the back of the cave, where his family has always slept all clumped together, but no eyes glitter back at him. While his ear ducts have lost their capacity to hear, his nasal passages, though severely hampered by his injuries, are still able to smell whatever lurks around him. But he cannot smell the presence of any of his kin. He cannot feel their bodily heat. It is as if they were never there, a dream, a false vision.

He turns and heads his way out of the cave, but not before bumping his broken muzzle once again, this time on a cold slab of stone. He stumbles clumsily out of the cave where the rest of the pack waits for him, huddled in a semicircle, some crouching, some gnashing their teeth, their muzzles stained red, all with their tongues pulsating out of their mouths, save for the one with the ripped-apart clump of furry flesh and broken bone dangling from its mouth.

The small, mutilated body that dangles—it is not a hare, after all, but something more horrifyingly familiar.

The great beast whimpers in the early sunlight, and lowers his face toward the ground. His comrades have already chosen what is best for the pack. When he looks up again, their cold, penetrating yellow eyes find his. The one with the youngest of the great wolf's offspring dangling from its mouth—their new leader—releases what is left to devour from the clutch of its teeth, and makes the first step forward. After his wounded predecessor belts out one last guttural howl up toward the morning stars above—his pain and anguish awakening the soul of every sleeping creature in the forest—the new leader lunges at the fallen giant, and with his ravenous comrades quick and eager to join him, begins to eat.

THERE WERE THREE of them by that stream over yonder—you might have passed it on your way over here. I didn't know what they was at first. It was early in da mornin and I'd been drinkin real hard the night before, so I thought, well, maybe it's my eyes again. Maybe it's my eyes up to their no-good tricks again.

They looked like—hey, you wanna know what they looked like at first? They looked like furry blankets—furry blankets that had been rained on with wet leaves all over them. I was thinkin, well, maybe it was some old campin site or somethin. But the thing about it was, what struck me a weird note about it was, was them flies. There were these flies swirlin round these wet and wooly things, and I was thinkin, well, maybe some folks had left behind some food and never came back for it—wouldn't be the first time we seen that happen around here. Folks litterin. Not carin for nature. Just treatin mother nature like a no-good cheap-ass whore they could jerk their weenies on. You've seen them folk. Come in from the city or one of them well-to-do suburbs just to do somethin they call roughing it. But us people living here, we're like, Hey, this is our home, man. This ain't some campin trip for us— this is our home. We live here. Do you throw your trash everywhere where you live, man? Well, maybe you do cuz maybe that's what you're used to in the city. But this ain't the city. This here is mother nature. This here is ours. This is all we ever known. Treat it with respect, goddammit.

Well, anyways, I got myself a closer look and it turns out it wasn't them city folks throwin their trash around—it was somethin else altogether. I mean, I couldn't believe it at first. All I saw was the eyeballs on one of them—the rest of what it was had flattened and congealed down to the ground like a furry, jelly pancake or somethin, and I wasn't sure if it was all one thing, until I got myself a closer look at the other two and they were in the same condition, their crazed yellow eyeballs of theirs staring up at me as if to say, Hey, motherfucker—don't you take another step now, ya hear? But it didn't matter anyway cuz when I saw them how they was, what they all looked like lyin by the water there, it made me hurl up good all over my boots. I mean, all them years I've been livin here, I've never seen one so close up like that, not even when they would come up to our ranch. But even though they were long dead, I was still frightened as hell.

Things like that worry me. Like maybe they are a sign of things to come in my life. And maybe everyone else's, for that matter.

You shoulda seen me though—came runnin out of dem woods like I seen a ghost, which in a sense I did, I suppose. Ran all the way to the house, swung open the door, and bolted right up the stairs. Forgot I still had all that puke on my shoes, speaking of litterin. My wife said ya could see my footprints all the way up to our bedroom, which is where she found me, cryin like a little boy who's seen the boogeyman.

She's a good woman, my wife. Cleaned all that puke up without sayin a single word.

But I never told her what I saw in dem woods—it was just too scary to even think about. In fact, you're the first person I ever told. Not exactly sure why I told ya—nor am I exactly sure how it would help your research and all, but somehow—well, somehow maybe whatever happened to Junior, whatever got into his mind and twisted it up—maybe those three bodies that I saw all clumped there and rotting—maybe that has something to do with it, and maybe that was the sign of things to come is what I'm sayin here, I guess.

I mean, I hope that's all that happens round here. I mean, there was that robbery up at the convenience store a couple of months ago, and then there was that old man who got hit by a jeep on the promenade there. But what I'm sayin here is, this whole story with Junior—it has created enough chaos as it is. We don't want people millin around this town forever—no offense to you, ma'am. Or you, sir. But the people in this town—we are private folk, yessir. We want nothin to do with what you folks in the city like to call the scene. We don't want to be part of any scene—we just wanna be left alone and live our lives the way we like livin them.

Besides, we got our own mayor to deal with, never mind yours.

———⊷◦C∕◦⊶———

MARE.

MAYOR.

Mare.

MAYOR.

Mare.

MAYOR.

Mare.

MAYOR.

THE EQUINE MEDICS had come and gone in their ambulatory van like ghosts in the night. Aside from the gaping one on her back, the mare's wounds had been deemed more or less superficial. The medics took pity on the horse and its owner, the latter who they surmised, from his own bodily condition and the condition of the farm on which he lived, was by no means able to foot the pecuniary cost of their endeavors.

Though having been told to bring his mare to the equine hospital once a week for a cleaning and checkup for the next several weeks, the man with the crooked nose has made the decision to take it upon himself to do all the cleaning and checking on his own. She is his, he reasons, and despite recognizing the medical context of the situation, there is something unseemly to him about another man's hands washing the various parts of her anatomy.

Doctors make him wary—even equine ones. It has always been like that for the man with the crooked nose, even before his beloved passed away.

Grace.

Gracie.

Grace.

There it is always. The pain.

He takes another swig from his flask, tucks it back in the waistband of his pants, and then grabs the bucket full of soap water. He wrings the cloth in the warmth of the water and reaches for the underside of his mare, soaking and massaging, the foam of the suds sticking to her hair in some areas, dripping and running down the slopes and curves of her body in others.

This thrice-daily ritual—he had been told by the medics to do it just twice a day, but who was to tell this doting horse owner how to care for his beloved mare?—is something the man with the crooked nose takes deep pleasure in despite the events that have caused it to be necessary. On some days, he prolongs the ritual to the point of there being no clear delineation between the first, second and third cleaning.

Today is one of those days.

After he finishes washing her underside, he massages the suds into her topside, squeezing the cloth over her back where the largest of the wounds are, watching the suds trickle down the flowing strands of her hair, hair untouched by the shears and razors of the medics due to his vehement objections, except in places on her body where access had been vital.

There is no getting used to the giant bite wound on her back. It is so gaping that, to him, it almost seems separate from her, its color changing daily. Today it looks to him like a purplish crater, a violent hole from which something erupted. He is no longer certain if it is healing or festering.

As he washes and rubs her backside, the suds from her tail flick onto his face, the foam dripping down the back of her hind legs.

That other hole that is behind her—he does not stare at it, only glances at it between swings of her tail. He feels it would be impolite to look at it for too long.

Somehow not looking makes the urge that much greater.

She never shows signs of protest. If she ever had, he reasons, he would never make such an overture. The way he sees it, as long as her body remains at peace as he performs, it is a benign act—Heaven permitting, that is.

After all, Grace is in there inside Gracie, isn't she? If she had not been in there, he would have never performed such an act.

Sometimes her tail sways during the act, with the foam still on it, tickling his thighs. This only stimulates him more, but sometimes it tickles him so much, it makes him laugh uncontrollably, and he ends up having to grab her tail to get her to stop.

But today, nothing makes him laugh, not even her sud-soaked tail brushing up against his groin—not with his own internal wounds festering inside him so.

Grace. Grace. Grace. Grace.

With the benign act having been completed, and his horse's backside now soaked in the suds of his own making, the man with the crooked nose lifts up his trousers, hops off the stool, grabs the bucket, and goes about his wringing again.

HOLD STILL, Gracie. Hold still, goddammit.
Good girl.

HE AWAKENS in the middle of the night to hear the sound of his beloved mare whimpering in the dark.

He lies there, on the floor of her stall, his head on a pillow that had been moved from the bedroom of his farmhouse.

He never sleeps in the farmhouse anymore. Not since the attack.

Everything all right, Gracie?

The man with the crooked nose listens, trying to distinguish the meaning of these sounds his horse is making on the opposite side of the stall: Is it her wounds? Is it a nightmare she is having? Is she seeing her attackers in her dreams? Can horses even have dreams?

Of course they can, he thinks to himself. This horse can, anyway.

He lifts his head from his pillow and crawls in the dark to where the whimpering sounds are coming from. After a half-dozen feet or so, he stops and puts out his hand to feel. As his hand makes contact, he feels the silky strands of hair. They feel almost human to him. He strokes the mare gently up and down, caressing her long neck.

Is that you in there, Grace?

In the dark, it feels too much like her that it must be her. He prays that the light would never return, that the illusion would never fade, that he would go on stroking her hair, seeing her face in his mind in the dark, the face of a sleeping angel.

A ray of light shines in front of his eyes. Is it the moonlight peeking through the cracks in the roof above? Or is it his true love sending him a message from the other side?

Before he can reach the tiny beam of light, it extinguishes, then reappears before him, its shape oval-like with moist cilia around its perimeter.

No, this is not a message. It is a light neither celestial nor lunar.

It is only his horse. Her head on its side, one eye staring up into his in the pitch-black of the barn. It is an eye glossed in terror. Her eye is open, but she is not awake. Something looms behind that eye that only she can see.

Her future.

His future.

His horse—she can see, she can dream.

He lays his hand back on her mane, and caresses her head, her ear, her neck. His fingers comb through her hair until the eye of terror recedes and all there is again is the stifling darkness between them.

THE SWARM has returned. Flashbulbs flash and boom mikes boom as a mustachioed man in a pinstripe suit welcomes the Great White Giant to the podium to deliver yet another benevolent proclamation. As the giant opens his mouth to speak, a hush comes over the swarm, its attention focused on the white glow of the solemn face before them.

In his whispery voice, he utters three words: The People's Banquet.

The People's Banquet, he whispers again. At the mayor's mansion. On the first Sunday of the following month.

The People's Banquet.

The People's Banquet, the swarm whispers back. The People's Banquet. They carry the three words with them back to their vast network of hives.

The People's Banquet.

Another moral act of goodwill for the benefit of the greater community. Another saintly edict for the masses to cherish and rejoice over. From news web to news web, from city block to city block, the three words spread and spread, over bridges, over mountains, over airwaves, to a small town up north where a short man with a long, crooked nose perched on a wooden bar stool watches the small television screen that is high up in the corner of an old and rundown tavern.

The People's Banquet, he whispers. The People's Banquet.

The words spin in his brain, interrupting the cycle of everything else that had spun prior. Gazing into the mirrored wall across the bar from him, he does not recognize the gaunt-faced man grinning back at him, nor the twinkle in his grayish blue eyes.

NOTICE TO VACATE — FINAL NOTICE

Dear Mr. [Last Name Redacted]:

We have recently been informed by a representative of our company that you, or a trespassing party that bears no association to you, have taken illegal residence on a property that has been legally foreclosed by one or more of our branch offices and has possibly engaged in an act of lewd and/or deviant conduct on said premises. As you might know, there are certain necessary measures our company must administer in order to physically secure any property that has been foreclosed under our company's auspices; your physical presence, or the physical presence of the unassociated party, on the foreclosed property in question has obstructed our staff from carrying out these measures. We ask that you or the unassociated party vacate the property immediately in order to avoid any unnecessary legal action, be it criminal or civil.

We appreciate your timely cooperation on this matter and wish you the best of luck in finding a new residence.

Sincerely,

[First Name Redacted] [Last Name Redacted]

Deputy General Counsel, Legal Affairs and Services — [Name of County Redacted]

[Name of Banking Company Redacted]

MARIJUANA NO LONGER works for the boy. Every time he closes his eyes, he sees his stepfather's giant hands reaching out to touch him, to caress him, to massage him, with mouth wide open, ready to swallow his small body from the waist on up.

His dreams are filled with whales with blowholes.

He ponders an alternative. He looks out his open bedroom window, and leans out.

He could jump. It would be a steep jump from the top of the mansion, but he just might land on his feet.

Or maybe he would not. Maybe his legs would collapse underneath him on impact, the pressure of gravity too much for his small body to handle.

Either way, it no longer matters to him. This was no way to live—he is quite young, yes, but wise enough to see the situation for what it is. His mother—she is not in the position. Her husband expects her to be in the same bed with him every night, no matter what violations he has committed against her and her only child. She just does not have the courage, the strength. She would never leave him. Fear now constrains her every action.

Perhaps she is old enough to get used to it. But not the boy. He has other plans for himself.

But what would be the plan? Where would he go? Who in this city would not recognize him, the son of the great mayor?

He would go up north. Over the bridge. Toward the mountains. Find a farm with a good family living on it—they could take him in, pay him for his labor. It would be the Christian thing to do. They would not ask any questions about who he was or how he got there or why he fled from the place he had once called home. They would not ask to know his past. They would see his face and already know he was racked with pain and damage—no need to ask him from what.

He does not want to be seen.

To be unseen—that is what he desires.

A farm, yes. That sounds right to him. With cows and chickens and sheep and other creatures of the world who would not judge.

Things that grow straight out of the earth, untainted—those are the things that he wants in this life. The things that would make him feel pure again, give him the room and the air to start anew.

All he has to do is make the jump.

He watches a bird perched on a slender branch outside his window. Freedom, like a bird's freedom—that is what he seeks.

He peers down at the front lawn of the mansion. The ground does not look so far down anymore. Flicking his joint from his fingers, he watches it descend, its sparkly tip floating its way gently down onto the freshly trimmed grass below.

He can make it.

She would understand.

Should he tell her where he is headed? Leave her a note? No. She's better off not knowing—her giant husband would only force it out of her.

But she would understand. She would know that wherever he was, it would be better than the situation he found himself in now.

And he would come back for her. When he earns enough of a living to call himself a man—yes, he would come back for her. He would make sure she is taken care of. Maybe she would move out there with him—some day, anyway.

The cool autumn air feels refreshing against his soft and fuzzy face. Closing his eyes, he sees himself neck-deep in a golden field of corn, with the big blue, wide-open sky everywhere above him, inviting him upward.

YA SEE THAT, Twinks? Ya see that squirrel I just shot? Now if someone had come by and seen me shoot it, would anyone blink an eye? Would anyone shed a tear? No, they would not. But if I shot a fuzzy, little fawn—would they care more? Or how about a cute, little dog such as yourself? Would someone raise hell about it?

Maybe then.

Perhaps.

But what if I shot a man? What then? And I don't mean in self-defense, mind you—I mean just if some fella came here wanderin about the property maybe—let's say deliverin the mail, or some groceries, or, okay, a foreclosure notice—would that get people going?

Uh-huh. It sure would.

Seems the higher we go up the food chain, the more corrupt the killing becomes. But should it not, dear Twinks, should it not be the other way around? Why is that mankind—and take note, dear Twinks, that I am sayin here mankind as opposed to humankind—why is that mankind gets all our sympathy, the ones with all the power at their fingertips, why is that they get all our sympathy when one of them gets shot, gets killed, gets hit by a truck, and not the harmless little ants we step on without even knowing it? Why is that when a movie star, or a politician for that matter, dies or gets killed it's a big deal to everyone, but when it's a homeless man on the street or the starvin child in some desert somewhere, they get no attention or out-pouring of sympathy whatsoever? I mean, if a homeless man—or a homeless woman, for that matter—was lyin still on the street corner, do ya think anyone would check to see if he was alive or needed any food or any water? No, they wouldn't—of course, they wouldn't. But if it were a mayor, let's say—if it were a mayor lyin there motionless on some street corner, would people stop to check on him? Would they get on their phones and call an ambulance? Oh, you better believe they would, yessir.

Why do we read about the man who gets hit by the train, but not the dog who gets hit by a bus? What makes the man more special than the dog? And while we're at it, what makes one man more special than another man? How come it is the powerful in their extravagant mansions who are protected by guards and not the hobo wasting away in his little cardboard hut? And why is it more taboo to shoot down the powerful man than the powerless one? Is it not more strange to wanna kill off that which cannot hurt you than the one who can?

See me skinnin this here squirrel, Twinks? I'm gunna make us a fire right out on the driveway here and I'm gunna sit back and watch it burn away. Then when he's all dark and roasted, I'm gunna take my knife and fork here, and I'm gunna eat the little son of a bitch. Now, if someone other than yourself here saw me doing all that—shootin him, skinnin him, cookin him, eatin him— would they lose a wink of sleep over it? Would they call the authorities, send an ambulance, call up the asylum and reserve a space for yours truly?

I think you already know the answer to that one, Twinks. But—and I bet since you're a smart, little dog, you know where I'm gunna go with this one— but let's just say, for argument's sake, dear Twinks, that if this were a mayor, let's say—not our dear mayor, mind you, but a certain particular mayor of a certain particular city—if he were the one spinnin around over in this fire in front of us, if he had been the one who had been shot down by yours truly, then skinned, roasted and eaten up until all that was left of him was his fat, filthy skeleton—well, that would be the story of the century, would it not?

Well, lucky for the mayor in question, we ain't breaking any taboos tonight—at least not this night anyhow. But I am sure you will agree with me, dear Twinks, that it is most peculiar how we pick what's taboo and what isn't—agreed?

Alright, Twinks. I'm done with my ramblin. You're a good sport for listenin. It's best we get to chowin down before the varmints come a sniffin. Here's a bone for ya.

WHAT DID YOU DO with my boy? says the brown woman with the chiseled cheekbones. I know you know where he is. Where is he?

The giant man scowls down at her with disgust, the late morning rain pelting the bedroom window behind him. I didn't do a damn thing to your boy. I'm as clueless to his whereabouts as you are. Probably went off with his friends somewhere. Boy stuff.

He ain't never not come home. It's been two days now, and you act like it's nothin. I know there is something wrong here. You better tell me where he is or—

Or what? The giant man looks at her crossly. Or what? You're gunna send some of your ole thugs from the hood after me?

You always wanted to send him off somewhere far away. Boarding school. Rehab. You was afraid he say somethin.

Say somethin? The big man runs his hand over his smooth head. Say somethin? What's he gunna say? Who would believe him? No one would. But what would you say if he did say something—that's what I wanna know. What would you say if he did?

She turns from the giant man and sits down on the bench at the foot of the bed. I need you to find out where he is. That boy—he's everything to me.

The giant man sits on the bench next to her, making it creak beneath them, and with its subtle unevenness with the floor, the woman feels herself see-sawing up ever so slightly. He puts his hand on her cheek and caresses it with the back of his large fingers. He bites his lip, his long, dark eyelashes aflutter on his glowing white face. The warmth she fell in love with so long ago has risen once again to the surface, but she has grown wise with time and knows what smolders behind the serenity of those deep, gray eyes.

I'll find your boy, he whispers.

IN ONE HAND, the man with the crooked nose holds the old-timers pistol over his head and aims it at the moon. In the other, he holds a tin flask, half-empty, its contents swishing inside with the shaky vibrations of his fingers.

Hello, Mister Mayor, says the drunken man to the glowing white ball of light above. It is a pleasure to finally meet you face-to-face. I have some things that I'd like to discuss with ya, some of them quite personal.

He takes a long swig from his flask, his gaze never wavering from the moon.

Now, Mister Mayor, I know you're a busy man, and so I won't keep ya too long, but ya see, I used to be a busy man myself, yessir. I used to transport some of your good, hardworkin constituents, as well as some of your most generous tourists, to and from some of your city's most-visited destinations and popular establishments, using what some would call a horse-drawn carriage, but what my ole colleagues and I like to call a buggy. Some of my prouder colleagues preferred the former term, but, me, I'm a simple man who likes to use simple words, so buggy suits me fine.

Another swig.

Now, Mister Mayor—and, by the way, I don't mind calling you Mister Mayor even though you are not my mayor and never was—now, Mister Mayor, I never made much money from my choice of trade, but I took great pride in it. It was a good, honest living—at least that's how I always saw it. I guess that's not how you saw it and those other elite members of your circle saw it, but that's how I saw it. Me and my colleagues—we were just good, honest, hardworkin men, minding our own business, just tryin to get by, but I guess you and your associates saw it in a different light—a political light, I presume. But this job I had—this right to make an honest living that you took away from me and shamed me for—it kept my days occupied, or busy if you will, as I said earlier. It kept my mind off of the things I didn't wanna think about, that I didn't wanna remember. Sad things. Dark things. Ya know, it's tough livin on a farm, all alone, with no one lookin after ya. It can drive a good man batshit—pardon my language, sir.

Another swig, then another. He shakes the flask—only a few drops left.

Ya see, Mister Mayor, the horse that used to pull my buggy—her name is Gracie, by the way—Gracie, she's in this here barn right behind me here. I'd let her out, but she ain't feelin so good these days. In fact, she's gotten herself mighty sick and can't hear nothin no more—ever since you banned her from the streets of your magnificent city, that is. I don't have the money now to make sure she gets taken care of, but she's not really what I've come to talk to ya about, no sir. No, what I really want you to know is that you took what was most precious to me—the love of my life, Grace. That's right, Mister Mayor. Because of your—how should we say it?—political audacity and alleged goodwill toward the equine species, I was not able to afford the treatment necessary to sustain her and our child who lived inside her. Ya see what I'm gettin at, Mister Mayor? Because of your political ambition and phony morals, I have lost everything I ever had or ever will have.

Now, Mister Mayor, I could shoot a bullet through my mouth and call it a day for all this pain and sufferin, but why do that now when I could shoot you right in the face first? But ya see, I haven't gotten there yet. I haven't gotten to that place in my mind that's needed for me to become a killer of men. That time will surely come, but it ain't here right now. Not yet. I haven't got the strength yet, the will, but it will come, Mister Mayor. My transformation— it will come, yessir. And when that day comes, Mister Mayor, I swear by God, I'm gunna point this here forty-four here right in your big, ugly white face and blow it all to smithereens, yessir. But first thing's first: I need some practice.

He turns his gaze from the moon, holding the pistol by his side, and gulps the final drops from his flask. A few yards in front of him, he eyes a tall tree stump next to the gravel driveway. He lays the empty flask standing upright on top of the stump and walks several feet backward, counting his steps along the way.

Eighteen, nineteen, twenty.

He cocks the pistol and squints with one eye closed.

Okay, you wily son of a bitch. What do ya think of them buggy rides now?

He pulls the trigger and the pistol fires. He feels the familiar empty rush of air gasping out of the barrel. It reminds him of his youth, when his old man let him aim and fire the very same pistol at the squirrels cavorting out on the front porch, before he was allowed to shoot with live rounds.

He lowers the pistol again to his side.

Dammit to hell. Where them bullets at?

THE BOY WALKS from one street to the next, from one avenue to another, the sidewalks and stoops filled with people whose skin are as brown as his, if not browner. Patrol cars are parked on every other corner, it seems, and every now and then he sees a street pedestrian, some as young as he, being leaned over the hoods of the patrol cars by white men in blue, their wrists handcuffed behind them, their african hair being squished hard on top of their bony heads as they are packed away in backseats, where they wait for one of the men in blue to wave an arm, to have them whisked away, the siren blaring, flashing off the windows of the rundown thrift stores and all-night bodegas like strobe lights at a raging disco.

The boy wonders if the giant man who has been designated as his father and the father of this great city has ever stepped foot in a neighborhood such as this, with its trash strewn on the pavement everywhere, its people scattered and shacked up in cardboard boxes and neglected tenements, huddled in groups of two or three or four over the nearest subway vent to keep warm, all with their pots and pans out in front of them, competing for the generosity of strangers who are perhaps a bit less deprived than they are.

The boy starts to think that maybe this is where he belongs—not in a mansion and not on a farm—but on the streets with the people of his kind, people who understand the cruel meanings of hardship and damage, and could use his help, his empathy, his influence.

These people, the boy says to himself inside his boy head, these people are my brothers, my sisters, my family. I will not ignore them. I will not look the other way. I will stay here and stand with them. I may not have been living the way they are living, but I know what it means to be forced and dragged into a life against one's will, a life that offers no hope and no way out.

He sees an old church, its doors and windows boarded, its window rails and metal crosses rusted out.

I will start there, he says. I will bring them back to having faith. In God. In the community. In themselves. I will build a city within a city. It will be a great city. It will take many, many years, but I will build it. God willing, I will.

A toothpick of a brown boy—a boy taller and older than he—wearing an oversized jacket covered in street grime, ambles in his direction.

Hey, you want one of these? the skinny boy says. In his shaky hand is a silvery gadget, its lights flickering in the night. It is something that the runaway boy does not need, but he knows this unfortunate soul peddling his shadow market wares has no choice but to get by any way he can if he wants to make it through the coming winter.

How much is it? the runaway asks.

The skinny boy names his bargain, and the runaway takes his offer, hands him what is in his pocket, then finds himself holding what seems, on its surface, to be a mint-condition device, not yet customized or authorized for everyday use. It is a sham gadget—its keypad useless, its screen flashing symbols in a foreign language—but by the time the runaway realizes this, the skinny boy has disappeared into the night's bustling herd and industrial fumes.

The runaway sees nothing personal in this small-time scheme, and shoves the faulty hand gadget into his pocket, ready to dispose of it at the nearest receptacle, but in a neighborhood where trash bins make for great campfires for those searching for warmth against the late autumn chill, he finds no such receptacle available.

A siren blares over his shoulder, its lights blazing a visible path in front of him on the dimly lit sidewalk. He walks only a half block more when suddenly he feels an invisible force crash against his spine, forcing his legs to collapse forward, his hands losing their freedom to maneuver in midair, his face crashing nose first into the pavement beneath him, the crack of bone in front of him, the clicking of metal behind him, the smothering weight crushing him from above, as the blue-uniformed bodies pile on top of his fragile brown back, flattening his body and splattering his blood across the cement.

Where'd you fuckin get this?

The runaway can smell the coffee-and-cigarette breath of the man asking the question, but with only one eye above the pavement, all he can see is the sham gadget in the confessor's hand in front of him. He cannot use his mouth to answer the question—not with his tongue bruised and his teeth scattered about him. Everything under his skin seems to boil toward the center of his face—if he moves it will all explode, he thinks. Best to lie still, a voice inside his crushed head thinks, but this internal suggestion is a moot one, for the half-conscious boy is unable to move even a single finger.

They lift his limp and shattered body off the ground, flatten his afro against his fractured skull, and pack him briskly into the leathery back of the patrol car. A man in blue with a metal badge on his chest waves his arm and the siren blares, sending the car screaming down the dimly lit avenue of this forsaken enclave of fatherless children, with no one turning their head around to even look—not even the skinny brown boy on the corner hawking the rest of his mocked-up gadgetry under the flickering spotlight of a shot-in streetlamp.

A MAN WITH a crooked nose stands in the moonlight in front of an old, red barn, a thin layer of horse manure covering his shaven scalp, his brown hands holding a long twine of hair, black and silky, that is not his own.

He gazes up at the moon, raising the twine of hair above his head.

Mister Mayor, says the man. Mister Mayor, do ya see this in my hands? This here is the start of my transformation. I suggest you make a note of it.

The man with the crooked nose carefully lays the twine of hair on the ground next to a pair of shears, pinning it down at one end with his foot to prevent the midnight breeze from blowing the twine away.

He cuts with precision. Strand by strand, he lifts the hair up and places it on his glazed and sticky head, starting at the center and working his way down the sides. His pace is brisk but purposeful, his shit-stained fingers kneading his scalp with the fastidiousness of a gifted ceramicist. By the time he finishes putting all the trimmed strands of hair on his scalp, there are none left to cover the back of his head, leaving it as bare and white as the moon above.

Here I am, Mister Mayor. What says you now?

He aims the shears like a pistol at the moon and pretends to shoot. Eager to see his new hairdo in the mirror, he turns and walks hurriedly toward the farmhouse. Halfway to the front porch, he hears his beloved mare whinnying in the barn, her muscular buttocks now naked and exposed to the cold night air.

I'D SAY HE'D come in here every other month or so.

Two months, maybe three.

He'd come in here and sit himself right down here in this swivel chair here you're sittin down in right now. I'd always ask him how'd he like it cut, and he'd say, Like so, and I'd say, Like so how, and then he'd show me how. Make his fingers into scissors, he would, and he'd show me.

Sometimes I'd ask him how he'd like it cut, and he'd say, No cut, just a trimmin, so I'd go on and give him just a trimmin then.

But whether I gave him a cut or a trimmin, it made no difference—he always fell right to sleep sittin right down in this chair right here right in the middle of it. The scissors—the snippin sound of them maybe, or maybe the feel of them against his hair—they'd put him in a bit of a trance, ya see, and then he'd go on and doze off right down in this chair right here. It'd be like one minute he'd be starin at himself right into that mirror there and the next minute he'd be fast asleep.

I remember this one time he came lumberin right in, drunk and stinkin as always, not utterin a single word. Just came right in and sat himself right down in this swivel chair here and fell right to sleep before I even got to cuttin. So I says to him, How'd you like it cut, but he says nothing back to me cuz he's fast asleep already, ya see? So I says it a little louder, How'd you like it cut, but he still don't hear a damn thing, his head and chin all down into his chest and everythin.

So then I got myself right up to his ear, real close, and I yell into it and say, How'd you like it cut, and you know what he did? He opens his eyes real wide and yells right back in my face and says, With dem shears goddammit, and just as soon as he yells it, and just as soon as I turn to grab them scissors, he falls right back to sleep with his head and chin all down in his chest again.

Sure.

Go ahead.

Laugh it up.

But you know what the sad thing about it was? This all went down when he was just a boy. Not even a teenager, he was. Just a small young boy.

A small boy with a big drinkin problem—that was Junior.

But a good boy otherwise.

Say, which side did you say you wanted that part on—was it this side right here or was it the other side?

THEY WERE TOLD to keep the room dim, if not dark, at all times. Too much light could give him migraines and aggravate his nausea. His mother sits at his bedside for hours each day, dabbing his forehead every half-hour or so with a cold compress, waiting for his chestnut-brown eyes to open and show the vaguest sense of focus or his bandaged-up head to tilt in her direction, but he never seems to fully catch on to her presence. They appear pensive, his eyes, at times, as if fixated on an object or idea within himself, but this seems more the byproduct of the pain medication administered than the glimmer of a recovering attention span.

The boy does not speak and lies in a muted, nearly vegetative, state for days, more likely due to the aftershock of the trauma than to the physical injuries sustained at the hands of the city's protecting class.

By the time he finally speaks his first word—Mama—and then delivers his explanation for why he ran away, his mother has heard more than she can bear.

A farm? she says. A colored boy workin the farm? That's what you wanna be? That's what all the blood, sweat and tears was for? So you can be some kind of slave workin the fields?

You must be some kind of goddamn idiot, says a bellowing voice from behind her. It emerges out of thin air from the dark shadows of the room, but the boy quickly picks up on its familiar tone.

It is he, the very monster of all his nightmares.

By the time the giant man with a moon for a face reaches his bedside, that feeling of dread that he had sought to escape from seizes his heart and mind once again.

See that, love, the man says. Told ya your boy was not right in the head. His goddamn foolishness will be the death of us all one day, I swear it.

He's just young, says the boy's mother. He don't know any better.

Ya got that right. He don't know shit. Just some dumb darkie with dark ideas in his head. Well, I got news for ya, boy—and notice I said boy and not son. You ain't no son of mine no more—let's make that straight. That charade is now over. But let me tell you somethin. If you were thinkin of going on out there and openin your mouth about me, you better goddamn think again. You will not see the light of day until every last bandage and every last stitch is out of that puny, little body of yours—you understand? Last thing I need right now is to go to war with the police commissioner. He and I have mutually agreed to keep this quiet, and we don't need something like this blowing up in our faces. We got bigger fish to fry in this city than worrying about you. In the meantime, your mother here, God bless her—she'll be the one taking care of ya. I told all the staff here to steer clear of your room. Can't risk that gettin out. Right now, everyone just thinks ya had yourself a biking accident, so if anyone asks ya now, ya now know what to say—got it?

The boy looks at his mother. Now that his eyes can see with clarity, she cannot bear to look at his pained expression. Just do what he says, love, she whispers.

The boy looks up at the giant man who never was his father. He wants to tell this man what he saw—the forgotten city within a city—but he is too weak to speak any further, and knows it will only fall on the deafest of ears.

I didn't hear an answer from you, boy. I said do ya got it?

The boy nods.

Alright then. The giant man turns and marches out of the bedroom, into the long, dark hallway beyond, his voice echoing down the corridor.

Working on a farm. A colored boy. Sweet Jesus.

OUTSIDE HIS WINDOW, the bankers hang from the branches of the hickory trees, their briefcases dangling from their bloodstained hands.

THE GIANT, moon-headed man watches the frail, brown boy in his child-sized bed, bandaged, asleep, and at peace.

We truly are all God's children, the man thinks to himself. Even the ones that do not follow His path.

The man walks slowly and deliberately into the boy's bedroom and quietly sits himself in the chair next to the bed. The boy breathes, sweet and calm, through his nose, his lips parted ever so slightly.

The man nudges the window drape open and sees the low-hanging crescent in the sky, its craters and contour as discernible over the city as one found in the picture books of small children.

Small children. So many in this city. All now sleeping sweetly in their beds, unaware of what lurks in the dark.

They need a protector. Someone to show them the way to God.

The giant man lets go of the drape and returns his gaze toward the boy.

He is not my child, but I can show him how to love someone else. We teach our children to read, to write, to swim, to ride a bicycle—why can we not teach them how to love?

The center of the boy's body rises and falls under the bed covers with every fragile breath, his bruised and swollen face the only part of him exposed to the elements of the room, save for the slightest hint of his brown foot sticking out from the bottom of the bedsheets.

His foot.

The giant man rises from the chair, ghost-like in the dark, then edges closer to the bed.

Such a boy. He does not know another way. A bastard child, he is. A fragile child grown more fragile.

Aglow in the dark stillness of the room, the giant man kneels down on the hardwood floor, next to the foot of the bed.

God delivers in mysterious and peculiar ways. This is this boy's deliverance. I will show him the light.

With his wide lips parted and suspended over the tiny toes of the sleeping child, the giant man waits for the right moment.

ON SUNDAY, a tiny black bug eats through one dead mouse. But the bug is still hungry.

—⋅⋅⋅⋅⋅⋅—

A MAN WITH a crooked nose walks halfway toward town, heading for the butcher's shop, when he hears the chimes of the church bell.

Sunday. The first Sunday of the month.

Oh shit, the man says, as he lifts up the brim of his hat and scratches at the dry manure on top of his head.

The People's Banquet. Time to get a move on.

He turns around, walks hurriedly back to the farm he calls home, and then begins to trot as he thinks about the next train departure time. As he walks toward the front porch of his farmhouse, a brown dog with a white undercoat stands up at attention.

Twinks, says the man. Today's the day. I need to get myself ready.

He runs up the stairs, to his bedroom, where he opens a closet door. On the top shelf he reaches for the wool overcoat that is balled up in the corner, an artifact from the old man of his old man. He remembers the last time he wore it—for a funeral service at church years ago—and puts it on.

Still fits.

He reaches back into the closet and takes out a small duffel bag. He opens it and then goes to a chest of drawers to pick out a change of clothes. After a minute or so, he turns back toward the bed.

No bags, he says to himself, no bags, and puts the duffel bag back in the closet.

What else?

Boots. I need them boots.

He walks back down the stairs and looks around the foyer, then the family room.

No boots there.

He marches back up the stairs, back to his bedroom.

Nope. No boots.

The man with the crooked nose heads back down the stairs again, out the front door, where the dog stands and wags its tail—for it never enters the man's house—and follows the man as he walks briskly toward the barn.

The man reaches the last stall in the back of the barn, where a horse stands diseased, deaf and catatonic, and finds his boots sitting overturned in the corner, its soles nailed in with horseshoes, caked with a thick layer of dried-up horseshit.

He begins to head out of the barn, the dog weaving in and out around his feet, when he realizes that this might be the last time that he will see or be seen by his beloved mare. He walks back toward the horse and strokes her muzzle.

Make it quick, he thinks. This is no time to get emotional. Besides, she is merely a shadow of her former self now, is she not?

Sweet Gracie. You be good while I'm gone, okay? Alright now.

He tips his hat at the horse and then marches out of the barn, dog in tow. He reaches the farmhouse, sits on the front steps of the porch, and slips his boots on. He stands up and walks back into the house.

The forty-four, he mutters.

He heads into the kitchen, reaches above the refrigerator, and grabs the pistol. He checks the cartridge and makes sure it is fully loaded. He opens a drawer and grabs more bullets, and begins to put some extras in his overcoat pocket, but then decides to take them out.

Hell, I'll be a dead man before I need this many bullets.

He tosses the spare bullets back into the drawer and closes it shut.

Forty-four.

Bullets.

Boots.

What else?

His eyes connect with something metal and shiny on the counter next to the sink.

The knife.

He grabs the knife, folds it back into the handle, and shoves it inside the side of his boot.

A perfect fit. Anything else?

Take a piss. Could be your last.

He goes into the bathroom next to the kitchen, pulls down his drawers and fires. Over his shoulder, he hears barking coming from outside through the screen door.

Gimme a minute, Twinks. Better yet, gimme five.

He turns around and sits on the toilet seat. Must be them nerves, he thinks. As he pushes out what is inside of him, he tries not to think too hard, but he cannot contain his excitement. He looks at the hunched and constipated figure staring back at him on the mirrored wall to the side of him and points a finger.

That's him, he thinks to himself. That's the guy. He's the one who's gunna kill the mayor.

A nervous grin begins to take over his face, but then quickly fades. His face is covered in brown. He has not bathed in weeks. He itches all over. His eyes are bloodshot beyond his years. The only thing he recognizes about himself is the trajectory of his nose.

Who is this man I see before me? Is he the same man he once was? Is he the same man who once loved and was loved in return by a woman of purest heart? And what happened to that boy he once was? The boy who shot empties at squirrels, who followed his daddy around the farm, watching him do the chores that farm men do? Where is that boy who watched his mother die right beside him? Is he still in there? Is he still down inside there lurking somewhere?

The dog barks again, this time louder and longer.

Hold on there, Twinks. Need another minute or two. We'll make it—don't you worry now.

He looks down at his boots. I should probably clean them up before I go so as not to leave any tracks, he thinks, but he knows that his timetable is too narrow to accommodate such an endeavor.

He sees the knife again on the inside of his boot. It makes him anxious just looking at it.

Best leave that here, he thinks. If it came to that, that would mean I did something wrong. Besides, the idea of shooting and fleeing felt more conducive to him than stabbing and then having to decide whether or not to stab again.

Having left the knife in the bathroom sink, he takes one last look around the first floor of the farmhouse, pacing from room to room, the dog still barking from the outside.

Okay, Twinks. Here I come.

He walks down the steps of the porch and the dog follows him around to the side of the house, where a rusty and rickety old two-wheeler sits on its side on a thin patch of grass and mud gone hard. He begins to lift it off the ground, but then just as soon, lets it fall from his hands.

Well, I'll be damned. Wait here, Twinks. Gotta go back and get myself one more thing.

By the time the man returns to the side of the house, cramming his tin flask into the pocket of his grandfather's overcoat, the dog has lifted its leg, creating a small cesspool of his own making next to the bushes.

Alright, Twinks, says the man, rolling the two-wheeler over the gravel driveway. I got about fifteen minutes to make it. I say I make it in twelve. Think you can beat me there? Bet ya can't.

The man with the crooked nose gets himself up on the two-wheeler and pedals off the driveway onto the dusty road that meanders this way and that, past a row of hickories, toward the first wooded extensions of the forest, the dog running behind him, trying to keep pace. Halfway to the woods, he realizes it would be easier to pedal if he were to take his boots off, so he stops to do just that and places the boots in the caged basket on the front of the two-wheeler. As he is about to get back on the two-wheeler, he looks over his shoulder and sees the dog sitting on its haunches, panting in the middle of the road, its tongue unraveled from its mouth, and behind his furry companion, the farmhouse he has dwelled in all his life, with the red barn he has so cherished sitting ghostly right next to it.

He thinks of Gracie, standing there in the dark in her own deafness, and a tear runs down the corner of his eye.

Gracie.

Grace.

Gracie.

Grace.

Onward he pedaled, up the main street, past the village square, the smell of fresh meat wafting through the open door of the butcher's shop as he rides by.

When he reaches the train station, no one is there, not even the vendor. He parks his two-wheeler against the wall of the station house, puts his boots back on his feet, and waits, pacing back and forth between the station's waiting benches and the edge of the boarding platform.

Three minutes to go.

Two minutes to go.

One minute.

Time's up—where's that goddamn train at?

He waits another five minutes, still pacing back and forth, leaning over the edge of the platform, hoping to see any sign of the train's approach, seeing only squirrels scampering about the steel rails of the track, when, once again, he hears the echoing chimes of the church bell.

Sunday. It is Sunday.

Then something explodes inside of his head like a firecracker: This station does not operate on Sundays, he remembers.

He takes his hat off and slams it onto the pavement of the platform. In an instant, a swarm of flies assembles to buzz around his shit-stained head.

Goddammit, Junior.

Goddammit, goddammit, goddammit.

I N T H E D A R K of the room, he feels a gentle hand, soft and warm against his face, waking him into consciousness. It caresses his cheek, his forehead—both no longer bandaged—and the hair behind his ear.

Mama, says the boy. His body shivers as the air blows through the vent above him.

The hand glides over his ribs and tickles him.

Mama, he says again.

He can feel the familiar fluttering on his abdomen, right above the waistband of his drawers.

It ain't Mama, says the man, with a giant finger to his lips. Hush now, boy. Be still and no one will get hurt.

The boy opens his eyes again and sees the glow of a moon bobbing up and down over him, the very same moon that has swallowed the center of his tender body for several nights straight.

This ritual of the night no longer haunts him the way it once did, for he has trained himself to sleep through it. With his eyes receding back into his head, his mind drifts back down into the womb of his inner world, into the infinite sea of wish and desire.

I'LL TELL YA what I always thought was peculiar about him—and I'm sure some of the others will have their own stories about him—but what I always found peculiar about him was that you'd never see him drive a car anywhere. Not even the one that was still parked in his garage after his old man passed away, may he rest in peace—not even in that one did I ever see him drive. And I think he sold that car—at least that's what I heard. But I mean, I don't think he even knew how to drive. Or maybe he did and just never showed it. And that—ya see, that to me was very peculiar. Very peculiar indeed. To be livin in these parts with no means of gettin from one place to the next—a grown man, mind you—well, that just struck me as a little odd. I mean, for a grown man to ride a bike as a way of gettin round—not even a motorbike, mind you, but just a regular two-wheeler—well, that seemed quite curious to me.

But, ya know, maybe that's an unfair thing for me to say. Not like his folks left him much money after they died. Pretty much left him bupkis and a mountain of debt is what I hear, and with the way that farm of theirs went to the crapper, it's not that surprising.

But going back to the bike for a moment—sometimes I'd see him ride it to the station here, and he'd leave it here till he came back from the city, and then he'd get back on it and pedal on home. Or at least I think he was going home—guess I couldn't know for sure. But most of the time—either on the way into the city or before he rode his bike home—he would order something from the concession counter here. Never a coffee or a croissant, but more like a bag of cheese doodles or a can of soder. Now let me ask ya: what kind of a grown man has a bag of cheese doodles and a can of soder for breakfast? And you shoulda seen how he'd drink from them soder cans—he would swish it in his mouth like a little toddler would and then swallow it down. And to me, ya see—well, that's why I sometimes used to think he was more like a child than a grown man. Now, maybe that was his old man's fault for not trusting him to ever do certain things around the farm and such. Maybe he was never taught to take the initiative, to go out into the world and find out what's he's good at.

But I guess what I'm sayin here is that when a man feels he can't go about doing the regular man sort of stuff—whether it's cuz someone's holdin him back from doing so or cuz he was never given the permission to at an early age—well, then that man will end up afloat in this world. A ship without an anchor, if you will. And then put that together with all that open space he had growin up and all those untamed beasts roamin around him—well, then things can really get messy. You can sort of understand how things might've gone awry for him and how he musta felt—um, what's the word I'm lookin for?—alienated from the rest of the world. And then having finally connected with someone—I mean, wasn't she lovely? Ya seen the pictures, haven't ya? Was she not a lovely young woman? But you can understand having finally connected with someone—someone of the opposite sex, okay?—you can see how that musta really kicked him in the gut, to have finally gotten somewhere and then seeing that all taken away right under that crooked nose of his.

Just sad, really, if ya think about it. I mean, that gave him no right to do the things he did, but at least you could maybe understand where he was coming from a bit more, why he mighta gone a little cuckoo. I mean, I've seen a lot of people—the same people—coming in and out of this station for so many gosh darn years now, but I have to say, even before all this stuff went down, he always seemed to be the most peculiar egg of them all. I'd be a liar if I didn't sometimes wonder if he would jump onto the track. I mean, I may not be the most educated son of a gun, but I'm smart enough to trust my instincts about people. And you can tell a lot about people from the way they talk, the way they walk, the way they travel, the way they eat, the way they sleep, the way they dress, the way they live. I know the way that boy—that man-child, I kind of wanna say—I know the way that fella lived.

It wasn't pretty.

His mama.

His old man.

It just wasn't pretty at all.

But in the end, who am I to judge another? Just some old fool sellin candy, coffee and cigarettes most his life. Not exactly grown-up stuff now, is it? But I'm okay with it. At least now I am. Feel like this is the way I fit in this world.

And that's important—to feel like you fit in, to feel like—oh, shit. Is that your train? Ya better hurry now and get on it. Was good talking with ya though. Enjoy the doughnut.

A MAN WITH a crooked nose sits on a wooden bench at an empty train station, his face in his hands.

What can he do? He has no car. He can borrow someone else's car perhaps, but it would raise too much suspicion. Besides, he has no friends to borrow from.

He has never had friends—not real ones, anyway.

He reaches into his pocket and takes out his flask.

A cab? No cabs in these parts. This ain't the city.

He takes a swig and then ponders on further. He contemplates riding his two-wheeler to the nearest operating station, but that would a good thirty miles away—his legs would never make it.

Guess it wasn't meant to be, he whispers.

He takes his boots off again, tosses them into the caged basket, gets on the bike, and begins to pedal.

He rides slowly back through the village square, back onto the main street, teetering this way and that as the whiskey kicks in, smelling the same meat smell he smelled on the way in.

As he makes his way out of the center of town, out through the stretch of dark woods, he sees the brown and white dog again, still on its haunches, its tongue still hanging from its mouth.

Well, I guess you remembered about Sundays before I did, Twinks, says the man with the crooked nose. As he pedals down the road, back toward the farmhouse, he can hear the dog panting behind him.

Reaching the driveway, he gets off the bike and lets it fall onto the gravel. He gives it an angry kick and then hops up and down wincing in pain as he remembers the boots sitting in its caged basket. He reaches for his flask again to ease the pain, but as he tilts the tin piece toward his lips, he hears a whinnying coming from inside the barn.

Gracie.

He tosses the flask in the air.

Gracie.

He cannot contain his excitement.

Gracie.

A madman under the sun, he dances a wild jig around the driveway, the dog barking giddily all around him, as if reading his very thoughts. After a couple minutes or so, he points his crooked nose up at the sky and gazes into the light.

Three o'clock.

Grace. Sweet Grace. We still have time.

YEP, I REMEMBER—it was a Sunday. Around noon, I think. Not a cloud in the sky.

I see him come walking—I musta been ten yards away from where you're standin now. Saw him coming up all alone—strange-lookin fella. Wore this big ole hat—couldn't really see his eyes too good. Dirty-lookin. Very dirty-lookin. Looked like he was covered in soot, like he had come out of an oven. Such an odd-lookin fella he was that there was no missin him. Was thinkin just some filthy farmhand passin through perhaps.

Well, about as soon as I spot him—and I don't think he ever saw me, by the way—but about as soon as I spot him, the church bells go off. That's why I think it musta been around noon—cuz of them church bells.

Anyhow, he hears them bells, and he just jumps up right into the air, I kid you not. Yep, he jumps up and then turns himself around and starts heading in the other direction. It was like them church bells scared the bejesus out of him, and he just took off runnin.

Strange, right? Well, it gets stranger from there—just you wait.

So, about an hour or so later, I'm sittin on my porch right here, just readin the paper, and guess who comes pedaling up the road on his bike, but the very same fella. And he was pedaling without his shoes on—I think he had them in the basket that he had on the front of his bike there. And he had this really big coat on himself too. But that wasn't what was strange, ya see. The bike—I recognized it right away. It was Junior's bike. The reason I knew it was Junior's was cuz it was like a kid's bike almost. He looked big on the bike, like Junior did. I was thinkin, whoa now, did that fella just go stealin Junior's bike? And then I was thinkin, well, maybe he's borrowin it or somethin.

Really, I didn't know what to think, ya see, but I figured it would be best if I just minded my own business and went on readin the Sunday paper the way I was. And, by the way, that's another reason I know it was Sunday—cuz of the paper. The only day I get the paper is on Sunday.

Well, anyhow, I figured that's that, there's nothin further to make of it, and I go about my readin. And I like to read a lot on this here porch here. I find it very relaxin. Especially on a Sunday. I like to read a lot of books too. I've read most of the popular ones.

Anyhow, I guess I was still readin away on the porch here. I think it was the one by that mystery writer—what's his name? Hell, I don't know. Doesn't matter. So, I'm readin here on the porch here, right—and it's like two, two-thirty maybe—and who comes heading back the other way on his bike—or whoever's bike it was—but the same strange-lookin fella with the big ole hat on his head. He was kind of riding much slower this time—couldn't tell if he was drunk or just enjoyin the fresh air or somethin. I was thinkin, well, for a guy who stole a bike, he sure takes it casually. So that sort of convinced me he was just borrowin it from Junior. And, by the way—Junior—he lives right down that same way. So, it sorta made sense to me—like maybe he had taken the bike out for a stroll or somethin and was on his way to givin it back to Junior.

But still strange, right? It's like then where's Junior in all this? Okay, well, ya wanna hear strange, I'm gunna give you strange like ya never heard it before.

So, around three-thirty, I'd say—yeah, that would be my best guess, three-thirty, maybe four—I'm about done with my readin. Yeah, I know—finally, right? So, I'm about done with the readin and get up out of my chair here—the very one I'm sittin here in right now—and start my way back into the house when I hear this sort of clip-cloppin sound cummin from way yonder down. Clip-clop. Clip-clop. It gets louder and louder. I'm like, what in the world is that?

Well, the first thing I saw was that dog everyone around here calls Twinkie. Cute dog. For a mutt anyway. Junior—he was the one who named him that, but that's a whole other story. So, the dog—Twinkie—I see Twinkie coming up the road, and for a while that's all I see, but the clip-cloppin, it keeps gettin louder and louder, so I shut the front door behind me and go walking down them stairs of this porch right here, up to the front gate, waitin to see what it was. I mean, I recognized the sound, sure—ya hear plenty of that sound around town—but never up this road. No, sir. But sure enough, there it was—a horse. And not just any horse, mind you—it was Junior's horse. And who was there on top of the horse riding her but that same strange fella with the big ole hat on his head. He was a grinnin from ear to ear, swiggin from one of them tin flasks—kind of looked like Junior's flask, but I didn't think of that till later on. But the horse—Gracie, that was Junior's horse—she just looked mighty awful. I mean, it made me real sad to see her that way. I remember the days when I would pass by Junior's farm and see that horse of his and she was a stunnin beauty, yessir, but the way she looked cummin up the road with that strange fella on her back—well, she just looked kind of old and sick. Blisters everywhere. They were festerin themselves mighty ugly. Her eyes too—they looked swollen shut. Poor thing looked about half-deformed I'd say. And her tail—I think it was clipped off or somethin. She wasn't moving well at all and seemed to be almost as drunk as the fella who was riding on top of her.

But it wasn't till later that I realized that musta been Junior himself riding her. I mean, he looked nothin like Junior. Like I said, his hat sort of covered his face, and he had all them heavy clothes on that didn't fit him right, so I didn't recognize him at all. Thought his hair looked mighty different too—at least from what I saw of it anyways.

I must admit though: I mighta had a few drinks myself that day. Yep. Nothin I like more than sittin here on this here porch here on a clear and sunny day with a good book in one hand and a beer in the other. I'm a simple fella, yessir. The missus might tell ya different, but don't go on listenin to her now, no sir. Hell, she likes to drink it up even more than I do, ya catch me? I mean, if ya wanna see somethin fucked up and strange, look no further than the lady clankin them pots right behind that winda there.

Around a mountain bend, on a descending and winding road, a man with a crooked nose on his face and an oversized top hat on his head rides a brown and weary mare, diseased and deformed and on her last legs, their canine traveling companion pacing a few yards ahead, ready to bark at the first sight of an incoming vehicle, but no such vehicle ever presents itself.

We're almost there, Gracie, the man tells his horse. Just a few miles more and I'll let you be.

He calls out ahead of him. Twinks? How ya holdin up? Ya need a drink? That pond I told ya about—should be coming up any minute now.

The daylight is in its final hour, but the sun is still quite strong for a late autumn afternoon. The brim of his hat and the motion of the horse keeps his head cool, but the man with the crooked nose can feel the heat baking him under his clothes.

They trot another half-mile or so, passing some of the tallest evergreens and boulders the man has ever seen, when, suddenly, the dog stops in the middle of the road, turns around and sits itself down on its haunches, its tongue hanging out from its black and drooling mouth.

Whoa, Gracie. The man stops his horse only a few yards in front of the sitting canine, then circles around the dog, giving it a good, hard look. What's the matter, Twinkie boy—had enough? I told ya—it's just another quarter mile or so before we reach the pond. How come ya lookin at me that way?

The dog lowers its body flat against the road. The man with the crooked nose looks one way, then the other.

Still no vehicles.

Hey, what's gotten into ya? Don't like what we're doing? Then head on back the way we came then. Good luck finding some water though—I don't recall seeing anything on the way down now.

The dog lifts up, whimpering, tilting its head to its side.

Oh, I know now. You think I don't have it in me, do ya? You think this idea of mine—it's just plain crazy, right? Here I am, just some hillbilly who's gunna come marchin into the big city and shoot down the mayor of all mayors. Is that it, Twinks? If that's it, then speak now.

The dog licks its lips and lowers itself back onto the road.

Nothin to say, eh? Look, I know what you're thinkin. You don't think I can kill a man, right? I mean, sure, I've killed squirrels, raccoons, cats, mice and even a wolf maybe, but that doesn't make me a killer of men, right? Well, lemme tell ya somethin, Twinks. Killin a man ain't no different than squashin an ant under your foot or smashin a mosquito with your bare fist. Ain't no different than killin them squirrels and raccoons neither. Just cuz a man can talk and write and dance and sing and pray and make the law, don't make him any better than the ant. No sir, it don't. I've heard the tiniest of creatures make such beautiful sounds with their mouths, it would put an opera star to shame. I'll take a chorus of cicadas over a chorus of choirboys any day of the week. A bird chirpin in the mornin. A cat meowin in the evenin. A woodpecker peckin in the sunlight. A wolf howlin in the moonlight. A mare moanin in the dark. I've heard each and every creature livin in these parts make the sweetest sounds on earth and I've killed each and every one of them, with my hands, with my feet, with this here forty-four right here down in my pocket. I've chopped down the prettiest of trees, tore out the most elegant of flowers. I've skinned a nose off a pig, cut the horns off a goat. What makes you think then that shootin a man—a loathsome, despicable man, mind you—would be any more troubling? Cuz he can reason? Cuz he can feel? Cuz he can love? Hell, you don't think a worm in the dirt can reason, feel or love? Or a pig in the mud? Or a mother bear in a cave with her cubs? Or speaking of ponds, how about them ducks? You think they can't reason, feel or love? Well, I've shot, killed, skinned, and cooked them ducks, so if you're askin me, Twinks, do I or do I not have it in me to be a killer of men, I think ya now know the answer to your question, yessir. Whoa, Gracie.

The horse jerks its head up and down, this way and that, almost stumbling off the side of the road before the man pulls her up by the reins and hops off her back.

Goddammit, Gracie. You givin up on me now, too?

The horse sidesteps off the road, onto the grassy shoulder, then lowers its body clumsily to the ground, her knee making a loud snapping sound as it lands. The man edges closer to his horse and sees the blood oozing from her mouth and eyes, the gunk spewing from her nose and ears, the bone sticking out of her leg.

Dear Gracie.

Dear Grace.

Grace, whispers the man. He looks at his horse, but speaks to a creature beyond. Oh, dear Grace, the love I always wanted only began when I met you. That cold and rainy mornin I found you on that bench, an angel stranded and drowned in God's tears—I remember that moment like it was yesterday. Not even your death has stopped ya from being in my every thought. It's funny how the memory of you can be so sweet but also bring so much pain. My love for you—it brings me strength but also a heaviness in my heart. The only thing that ever felt pure to me in this world was that love we had for one another, and it burns me up inside to know that I will never again be able to share that with you, to feel your hand in mine, your skin against my skin, your lips against my neck, your whisper in my ear. You made me feel so alive—my body, my mind, my spirit—that I had no reason to hurt or kill anything. But with you now gone I feel I haven't a reason to go on. It's like I just feel so dead—like a ghost in the woods. But I feel betrayed too. Like what I had didn't just blow away in the wind but was taken from me. Taken by the worst kind of evil ever inflicted on this earth: a man who says he is the man of the people but who is anything but. He inflicts pain and sufferin on other human beings, but does so with words and ideas and laws that no decent god would ever condone. He is a predator of the weak, of the poor, of the downtrodden. He has hurt good people, honest people, and taken away their hope, their dignity, their means for makin a livin. He lives in a mansion to end all mansions while the good people of his city fight over the scraps. He has left me with nothin but the rotten feelin of vengeance inside. He has taken away my livelihood, my child, my beloved, and now, soon, my horse, and I shall avenge this carnage. But I am sorry, dear Grace. I cannot push forward with you watching over me. I now must put you to rest.

The man with the crooked nose puts his hand inside the inner pocket of his coat, pulls out his pistol, and aims it at the horse.

Goodbye, sweet Grace. I love you. Always and forever.

The dog barks, then growls, then barks again.

Goddammit, Twinks. You can turn around and leave or you can stay and watch me be the killer that I said I was. It's your call.

The dog whimpers and squeaks. It takes one step forward and looks into the man's eyes.

Last chance, says the man, but the dog has already turned around, trotting at a hurried pace, looking behind every so often until the man and the horse are out of sight. After a quarter of a mile, it stops in the middle of the road and sits on its haunches, facing the direction from which it just came, its tongue unraveled from its mouth. It waits there for a minute or so, then gets up and takes a careful step forward, then another, but before it puts a paw to the road again, it hears the gunshot, sending it swiveling back around and sprinting as fast as it could go, up the ascending and winding road, around the bend, always moving forward, never daring to look back again, its mouth drooling and panting, the fresh mountain air blowing through its straggly coat of brown and white hair.

LET ME BE clear: I've done some awful things in my life. It took me a long time before I found salvation in our Lord. My family and friends had all but abandoned me when I hit bottom. I'm not gunna sit here and rehash past sins. I've confessed them all to the Lord long ago already. My priest got his earful from me—yes, he did. Besides, the Lord—He sees everything all the time anyways, does he not? Of course, He does, yes. So, I don't mean to gloss over my past—not that it's any of your business anyways—but you should know that I put my faith in God after turning my back on Him for so many, many years. I wish I could say why I turned my back on Him—maybe it was how I was raised, maybe I never had the proper guidance, maybe I didn't love myself enough, who knows?—but it was probably for not any single one reason is what I'm sayin here. But when the mayor—not our mayor, mind you, but the big one, the one from the city—when I saw him, the mayor, for the first time on the teevee, and when I heard his story of how he was not always as righteous as he shoulda been when he was young, that he had violated God's will and had asked for His forgiveness, it moved me. I saw myself in him. Ya might laugh at that, seeing the way I live here and the way I'm sure he lives the way he lives where he is, but it made me—what's the word?—reassess my place in this beautiful world God has created for us.

Look, I was never a people person. Not sure if I still am, but I try to do the right thing whenever I can. When I was driving on the road that day, and saw that shadowy figure standin out in the distance by the side of the road with his thumb in the air, believe me, my impulse was just to keep on truckin, don't stop. But, like I said, I know what the Lord expects me to do, and I will never go against His expectations. Love thy neighbor, He says, so that's what I did. And it was tough stayin on that path in that moment, for this man, when I pulled up next to him and he walked up to the passenger side winda, he looked less like a man than like somethin else. I'm not sayin he looked like some cross-dresser or nothin—though sometimes I wish he had been so I could have sped right by him with no sense of guilt, ya know—but he looked more like a creature or somethin than like a man. A giant insect, ya might say, rather than a small man, which was what he was, of course. But when I saw that sadness in his eyes, and when he pointed to his horse lyin there dead by the side of the road, how could I have said no to him?

When I rolled down the winda, he didn't say hi or even wave hello. No, what he said was—and I remember this very clearly—he said, I just shot the mayor, and I said, Come again, and he said, I just shot my mare, and I was like, oh, that's what he said then. But now I'm wonderin if I heard it right the first time. Like maybe he did one of them—what do they call them?— Fredonian slips? Or maybe it wasn't one of them slips, just a message from above that I wasn't prepared to decipher. And sometimes, when I look back on it, it just makes me feel sick inside—like maybe I could've done something about it, like maybe I had a sneakin suspicion about him and I could've done something about the whole thing.

Well, even after he tells me he's headed for the city, he didn't even ask to get in the car right away—no, he didn't. No, what he did was ask me if I had a blanket by any chance. He didn't look chilly to me and it sure was a hot one that afternoon—for late autumn anyways—so I didn't know why he had asked me for one at that moment. It was not until we got on the road and I thought about it that I figured he probably wanted it to protect his horse's carcass from the elements, ya see.

He didn't say much in the car. Said he was headed into the city to meet a friend—wanted me to drive him to the nearest train station. Sure, it was strange for a man with a dead horse on the side of the road to be all of a sudden heading into the city to meet anyone, but I figured it was none of my business, and I could tell he didn't wanna make it so. Asked him his name, and though he gave it to me, I didn't believe for a second it was his real name. He had never asked for my name, but that that didn't occur to me until after I had dropped him off, and I'm not so sure I woulda given it to him either even if he had asked for it. I'm not sayin he looked dangerous or nothin—like I said, he was a small man, like an insect—but it was clear something was not right about him. I mean, I'm not entirely sure if this was so since my eyes were mostly on the road of course, but I think he had these metal things— looked like horseshoes or somethin—stuck onto the soles of his shoes. Don't recall ever seeing something like that before. He also had himself one of those ole-fashioned top hats on his head, if you can believe that, like if he were from some other era or somethin. And his hair—I don't think it was a wig or nothin, but it didn't look like his own. In fact, whatever that was under his hat, I'm not so sure it was human even—at least, not the ponytail-lookin part of it. Even the scruff on his face looked like it was pasted on him.

And what was also sorta weird was that I remember him askin me—no, tellin me—to turn the radio off. Said, Please turn that off—just like that. Very weird, right? Very weird indeed. But guess who that was talking on the radio when he told me that: yep, the mayor himself—the big one. But what did

I know then, right? I mean, the way he looked, the sadness in those droopy eyes of his—sorta bloodshot, they were—and with what happened with his horse and all, what else could I do but turn it off? So that's what I did—I turned it off. Felt it was the only Christian thing to do.

But like I said, he didn't say much, so I didn't learn much about him until later when everything went down the way it did. But even now it doesn't sound like anyone really knew him really. Kind of made me think about myself though, how I used to be. Made me wonder if anyone really knew who I was when I was the way I was. Truth be told, I'm not sure anyone knows me fully even now, except for Him. But I think it's safe to say that he never turned to face the light of God the way I did though, but I guess that's pretty damn obvious. Me, I just try to be a good person and do the right thing, to be kind to others in need—and that's what I did when I let him into my car. I'd be lyin to ya if I told ya that this whole thing didn't make me question my faith, but maybe there is some larger good here that folks like you and I just can't see right now, but will see when the time comes for Him to want us to see. I mean, what happened—well, it just breaks my heart. Ya already know how I feel about that mayor, so you can just imagine. But I can't take responsibility for another man's evil actions—we all have to be responsible for ourselves and the ones we love. I know that now. Now that I have God in my life, yessir.

Hold still, Twinks. Hold still, goddammit.
Good boy.

OH, TWINKIE? I don't know when or where that dog came from. They used to—Junior's family, I mean—they used to have their own farmhouse dog, a different dog from Twinkie. Devildog they called him. He was anything but the Devil though. Cute little black thing with a red bandana around its neck—ya know, classic farmhouse type. Wasn't much for herding though. But the boy—Junior, I mean—that's what everyone calls him around here—Junior—he loved that dog, yessir. Always was with him when he walked into town. A sweet dog, that dog. Someone said his old man shot him, but I never believed it. Think he just came down with somethin and they put him to sleep.

But, Twinkie? Yeah, he belonged to no one, really. He was a brown and fluffy little mutt. Looked sort of like what a farmhouse dog should look like, but I'm not sure if he ever truly was that. He musta belonged to someone around here at one time or another since he was never rabid or nothin. Nah, he just kind of roamed from farm to farm. Sorta like the town dog, he was. I once saw him come wanderin into my shop right through that front door right there all by himself. I offered him a biscuit, but he wasn't interested. Started peeing on a stack of newspapers I had right there on the floor there. Told him to get the fuck out. I felt bad for sayin it—him being the sweet dog that he was—but I couldn't have him doing that to my store.

I didn't see him anywhere for a while after that—this is before he went by the name Twinkie, by the way. It wasn't until I saw him hanging around with Junior a lot—they were always coming into town together—that I heard anyone call him Twinkie. Junior was the one who started calling him that and pretty soon after that, so was everyone else.

Yes sir, Twinkie. Ya know those old tasty cakes they used to make—Devildog and Twinkie? Well, now you can understand why he called him that—first there was Devildog, then Twinkie. Thought it was pretty funny of Junior, actually.

Oh, that Junior. Ya know, after his woman died—Grace, I think her name was—after she died I didn't see much of him and that dog together, no sir. In fact, I didn't see much of Junior, period. And when I did see him it was like he wasn't himself—always drunk like his old man was. His mama, too. A family of drunks—the three of them.

Anyhow, I hadn't seen Twinkie for a while until the afternoon of the incident in question. He just came wanderin in through that front door just like he did the last time. I said to him, Twinks—are ya gunna piss all over my papers again or what? But he didn't piss on nothin, no sir. He just kind of stared at me and whimpered some. Looked sad, really sad, like he was depressed or somethin. Very tired-lookin too, like he had walked or ran some great length. I let him mope around until the end of business hours, then told him to skedaddle. Thought about lettin him sleep overnight in this here shop, but I was afraid the place would be drowned in piss and poop by sunrise. I mean, I guess I coulda taken him home with me like some of the other shopkeepers around the neighborhood, but the thought never really occurred to me at that moment. I don't know—guess I'm not much of a dog person.

Anyways, that was the last time I've seen that dog anywhere—that afternoon, I mean.

Yep, Twinkie and Devildog. That was them alright. Cute little critters, the two of them were—in their own respective ways, I suppose. Good dogs too, yessir—regardless of the vices of those who named them, that is.

Say, ya know what? That reminds me. We got some of them new yodels on the rack in the back corner there, if you're interested. Ever have one of them? They're mighty tasty, yessir.

THE LINE WRAPS AROUND for dozens of blocks. Men, women and children, some in groups, some as couples, some alone, all rubbing their hands together in the chilly late autumn evening, the sun having bid an early farewell.

Up in the sky, the crescent moon offers its sideways smile to the city's forsaken and forgotten.

As the homeless await their chance to enter the giant gates of the great mansion, volunteers in aprons hand them slices of sweetbread and small cups filled with warm apple cider. Every ten minutes or so a man's voice on a distant megaphone blurts out a welcome for the next few dozen of the city's impoverished to proceed forward and enter into the mayor's front garden.

In the middle of this long line stands a man of short stature, his face gaunt and scruffy, his nose smudged and crooked, his hands stuffed in the pockets of a worn-out overcoat, his head covered by an oversized top hat and tilted downward toward the concrete of the sidewalk. His fellow members of the peasantry standing directly behind him give him a good five yards or so as they cover their noses with their hands to block the toxic aroma of fecal matter emanating from the top portion of the man's concealed head.

A gummy old man in a tattered overcoat of his own stands in front of the malodorous peasant, hunched over at a similar height, muttering to the pavement, paying no heed to the infectious stench coming from behind him.

Keep it coming, keep it coming, blares the voice on the megaphone, its decibel rising higher and higher as the line moves farther and farther forward. Under the brim of his hat, the man with the crooked nose can see the policemen lined up and down the avenue, diverting and blocking off all traffic, their black pistol butts jutting out and jostling from the sides of their holsters. His eyes dart from one officer to the next, his shoulders shivering under his overcoat.

One of these men might shoot ya dead tonight, he thinks to himself.

Let's go, let's go, says the voice on the megaphone.

The man with the crooked nose puts his hand to his chest. His coat is so thick that he cannot feel the pistol inside it. He wonders if it is still there, or if he had unknowingly dropped it on the train on the way in—or, even worse, in the car of the man who had driven him to the train station—his fingerprints all over its handle.

He imagines one of the officers pulling him aside and showing him his pistol: Looking for this?

The line speeds ahead. The man with the crooked nose can now see the mayor's mansion through the fence. He counts the windows across. Sixteen windows. Three levels high, plus what appears to be an additional half level.

Probably an attic, he figures. He tries to picture himself climbing into one of the attic windows.

Keep it coming, keep it coming. Stop.

He sees the black and golden rails of the gate and the dark-suited men standing in front of it, their earpieces snug in their ears.

Almost there now—just one more batch of peasants, and I'll be through the door.

The minutes move ahead at a glacial pace, as the doubts inside his head begin to fester. Too many policemen. Too many men in dark suits. Too many people milling about—I'll never get close. Maybe I'll never even see the son of a bitch.

Okay, next, shouts the voice on the megaphone. He can now see the owner of that voice, a stocky man in a short-sleeved button-down, a clipboard tucked under his armpit. It reminds the man with the crooked nose of the banking rep who trespassed his barn a few months back.

Gracie.

Grace.

Gracie.

Grace.

A young homeless man wearing a washed-out baseball cap and a coffee-stained sweat jacket is stopped in front of the gate. A security guard with a tie peeking out from under his windbreaker pats him down with a body scanner, as the young man lifts up his arms.

The scanner beeps.

Empty your pockets, sir, says the security guard.

Several coins come jiggling into a plastic container, followed by a small folded-up pocketknife.

The man with the crooked nose thinks about his own folded-up dagger sitting in his bathroom sink. His sweat grows thicker.

What do you need this for? says the security guard.

Come on, man. I use it to cut fruit and stuff, says the young homeless man. Shit like that, ya dig?

Alright, says the security guard. When you leave tonight you can pick it up here on the way out. Next.

The old man in the tattered overcoat shuffles forward, still muttering to the pavement. It makes the man with the crooked nose think about his grandfather—a man he never met before, but whose old coat he wears tonight.

The old man mutters away, and the security guard with the scanner looks at the one of the dark-suited men. The man in the dark suit steps forward to confront the old man, but the old man continues to talk in gibberish, though louder now, still keeping his eyes to the ground and never once looking up at the man addressing him.

Sir, can you step this way? says the man in the dark suit, but the old man only speaks gibberish louder and louder, as if shouting to a child no one can see.

Sir?

The man lifts his head and spits on the tie of the man in the dark suit.

Okay, pal, come this way. The man in the dark suit whisks the old man away, across the avenue, toward the opposite sidewalk where other members of the peasantry pace back and forth in congregation, talking and shouting to invisible companions whom no one but they can see.

Okay, next.

The man with the crooked nose steps forward. He knows they got him. He lifts his arms without even thinking, for there is nothing else he can do. There are too many men in dark suits to stop him if he just cuts and runs—that would just further raise their suspicion. He is surrounded—the mayor's men have him boxed in. As his arms go up at his sides, a beggar ready to be crucified, the security guard raises his jacket over his nose.

Whoa, partner, says the guard. Alright, let's do this quick now.

The scanner combs over the reeking visitor, and the beeper goes off.

Alrighty. Let's take a look and see what ya got inside the coat there.

The man with the crooked nose shrugs his shoulders. A good man knows when he's been had.

The guard gestures to another man in a dark suit, who taps his earpiece and then stands in front of the man with the crooked nose. He feels up and down with his palms, then sticks his hand inside the overcoat—its wearer now praying inside his head with his eyes closed—and pulls out the rusty metal.

I'm sorry, says the man with the soiled head. I can explain.

The man in the dark suit dangles the metal piece in front of the visitor's crooked nose and hands it over to the security guard. See that?

The man with the crooked nose opens his eyes and sees his tin flask glistening under the sidewalk lamp.

The man in the dark suit looks back at the shaking visitor. No drinking allowed on the mayor's property, you understand?

Okay, buddy, says the guard, his jacket still over his nose. You can go on through now.

ON A CLEAR and starry night, a weary mixed-breed of brown and white lumbers and whimpers his way out of the woods, onto a dusty, winding road, weaving this way and that way, past a row of hickory trees, until he reaches an old, broken-down farmhouse. He scampers up the porch steps of the house and waits for its sole occupant to return home, his belly and jaw flat against the porch floor, his brooding face sandwiched cutely between his two front paws, facing out toward the road he has just traveled.

As the night's darkness grows thicker, he listens with quiet intensity for the sound of feet against pavement, against rock, against gravel, but hears nothing. After the minutes and hours have accumulated more than he can bear, his pointy ears fold back onto his head, as he drifts off into a heavy slumber, unimpeded by the nighttime chirping and buzzing of crickets and cicadas.

But he is not alone. Coming onto the porch, rising up between its wooden planks, no bigger than a baby's first tooth, is a tiny black crawler of the night. When it sees the fluffy brown and white heap in its path, it stops in its tracks, and whiffs the air.

Hair.

Meat.

Bone.

Blood.

It is all there.

The tiny black crawler remains still and waits for several minutes. Convinced that its prey is asleep, it creeps quickly over the next plank and reaches with its leg for the outermost strand of hair on the furry creature's tail. Hoisting itself up onto the tail, it quickly scurries up the dense forest of brown tufts until it reaches the mutt's anus.

The tiny black crawler takes another whiff.

This is the way in.

It takes another deep breath, shaking its entire micro body to its core, then burrows its way headfirst into the dark and narrow hole, secreting speckles of venomous saliva from its mouth to moisten out its path as it pushes on forward.

The straggly-haired canine stirs in his sleep and wags his tail. Behind his closed eyelids, he looks on at the man with the bloodshot eyes and crooked nose whose pistol is cocked and ready.

THE WAITERS and waitresses seem to come from every direction, their black bowties covering their necks, their white button-down shirts neatly pleated, their hands holding up trays filled with tiny morsels of various upscale meats on toothpicks.

Hors d'oeuvres for the homeless, mutters the man with the crooked nose. How quaint.

In the middle of the garden are rows of tables, each serving its own culinary category: pasta, cold cuts, poultry, beef, seafood, vegetables, pastries, ice cream, tea, cocoa—it goes on and on. The homeless hordes form orderly lines around the tables of food and await their turn for the table server to fill up their plates.

A hobo holding a drumstick in one hand and a chicken kebab in the other points over his shoulder and tells the man with the crooked nose to try the duck.

It's right over that way. Best damn duck you'll ever have—believe me, brother.

I believe ya, says the man with the crooked nose. But he is not hungry. He has not been hungry for days.

Statues and busts of mayors and city officials long gone are scattered about the property. A gigantic metal sculpture of tangled torsos and limbs captivate the impoverished onlookers as they chomp up what they hold in their hands.

I think that's supposed to be his heart right there, says one woman.

Nah, that ain't his heart, says another. That's his head. He's bendin down there, ya see?

A bronze statue of a celebrated general on horseback from the old country stops the man with the crooked nose in his tracks for a moment, as he ponders its personal significance. He then weaves his way around the various monuments, until he comes upon a circular throng of transients several rows deep, many of whom stand on their tippy toes, observing whatever it is they are surrounding.

The man with the crooked nose walks by the circle of peasants and tries to catch a glimpse of what is being witnessed, but he knows he has no chance for he is still a man of diminutive stature, even with his horseshoed boots on.

As he rounds the circle, his eyes spot an empty food crate under an unused serving table just off to the side of the crowd. He grabs the crate, places it about a dozen yards away from the circle, and stands on top of it.

There he is. The white devil in the flesh. His head giant and glowing in the night. The crowd of peasants encircling him listens with rapturous attention as he speaks with whispered inflection, as if he is delivering them a secret straight from the Lord Himself.

You are God's chosen people. You will find salvation if you walk in His footsteps. Lay down your suffering and lift your face toward the light.

The man with the crooked nose presses his hand down hard against his chest. The forty-four—it is still there. He wonders if this is his moment, if this is his time to do what must be done. Seeing his hands shake at his sides, he puts them in his pockets.

Shooting from where he stood would be too difficult. He might end up shooting someone else in the crowd by accident.

This is not the time.

Something small taps him behind the knee, making it buckle for a moment.

Hey, can I get a look there too?

The man with the crooked nose looks below and behind him and sees a small, brown boy with buckteeth wearing a hooded jacket and corduroy pants with a hole where the knee is—both too short a fit for the child, his white athletic socks sticking out above his mud-stained sneakers.

Do ya mind, sir?

No, I guess I don't.

The man gets down from his perch, and the boy heaves himself up on the crate, holding his nose.

Shit, man—you really reek, says the boy.

Don't I know it, says the man with the crooked nose. Maybe the mayor can let me use one of his bathtubs.

Well, he's got at least five in there, that I know.

How ya know that?

The boy gets down from the crate. I can't see shit. What's that ya say?

I said how ya know that—about them bathtubs, I mean.

Cuz I've been in there—he's showed me some of them.

Who did?

The mayor. Who do ya think?

Stop pullin my chain, kid. I ain't as gullible as I look.

I ain't pullin nothin on ya. I'm tellin ya the truth. In fact, I'm supposed to be seeing him tonight, after the banquet.

Oh, really now. Tell me—what for?

I do favors for him.

Favors? What sort of favors?

Ya know—favors. Housework sort of stuff. He pays me for it.

What would he need you for? Hasn't he got his own butlers and maids to handle that sorta thing?

Yeah, but he likes helpin out us kids. Us orphan kids, I mean.

You an orphan?

Uh-huh.

Me too.

Really?

More or less. And so was my woman.

Wow. So where's your woman now?

The man points to his head. Up here. Then to his chest. And in here.

The boy scratches his head, looks down at the ground, then back at the man with the crooked nose.

The man with the crooked nose looks down as well, then back at the boy.

Well, uh, hey, listen, kid. I gotta piss like there's no tomorrow. It's been nice shootin the breeze with ya and all, but I gotta get myself to one of them portal potties over there.

Maybe you can do some favors for him.

Come again?

I said maybe you could do some favors for him too. You being an orphan and all, maybe he'd help you out too.

He won't want none of my help. I ain't a kid like you are.

No, but you're short like a kid.

Yeah. I guess so.

So you want me to ask him then?

When would ya ask him?

Later tonight. When he comes down to the cellar to see me and the other boys. I've brought some of my other friends who are orphans to the cellar and he don't mind having them around. As long as they do what they're told, he don't mind payin.

You said the cellar—what cellar are ya talking about?

It's in the back. It's been turned into this underground home for me and the other orphans. Me and the other boys—we sometimes call ourselves the Lost Boys. You know, like those boys in that book with the pirates in it? Come on—I'll show ya. You can piss there. It's got a bathroom, and even one of them bathtubs too, if ya could believe that.

The man's heart beats faster and faster. He puts his hand inside his coat to calm its rhythm, his hand brushing up against the butt of the pistol inside.

He looks at the boy, a brown angel in the great green garden, and nods his head.

Okay, says the boy. Let's hurry up quick before ya wet them pants of yours. And who knows? Maybe if he takes a liking to ya, he'll let ya take a bath in the tub like he lets me and the other boys do.

A bath, eh?

As he follows the boy around to the back of the mansion, the man with the crooked nose hears the circular congregation applauding behind him. Holding his coat tight at the chest, the late autumn breeze nipping at his cheeks, he imagines how it would feel to be naked and victorious in the bathtub of his slain enemy.

HOLD IT steady now, Junior. Hold it steady, goddammit. Goddammit, goddammit, goddammit.

THE BROWN BOY with the buckteeth leads the man with the crooked nose to the back of the mansion, past a security guard who nods his head at them.

What the heck was that? says the man with the crooked nose. Isn't he gunna stop us?

Why would he do that? says the bucktoothed boy. He knows who I am. And he knows I bring new orphan kids with me here all the time. You so short he probably thinks you one of them too.

The boy leads the man to a set of stone stairs that spiral down to a black iron door.

At the bottom of the stairs, the boy knocks on the door. After knocking for more than a minute and getting no response, he starts to walk back up the stairs, the man in tow, when the door creaks opens below them.

Hey, where's you going? It is another brown boy, similar in size and proportion to the first brown boy, only his mouth is more snaggletoothed than bucktoothed.

Oh, hey, says the bucktoothed boy. We was just coming to drop by. My friend here wants to do some of them favors for the mayor.

The snaggletoothed boy looks the man with the crooked nose over with suspicion. This white boy—how you know him?

He's an orphan like we are, says the bucktoothed boy. He needs to take a piss real bad, so give him some room.

The brown boy with the buckteeth leads the man with the crooked nose through a maze of bare sheetrock corridors, the lighting fluorescent above their heads, before coming upon a room full of other brown boys, stoned and strewn across the unsheeted mattresses in a dank and dimly lit room.

Shh. Keep quiet, says the bucktoothed boy. The bathroom—it's over there. There's a bathtub in there too if you wanna use it.

The man with the crooked nose enters the bathroom and relieves his bladder, not paying any heed to the rusty white bathtub behind him.

He is a king grown comfortable with his crown of aged horse manure.

As he drizzles into the toilet below, he feels a draft against the side of his drawers and realizes he is standing next to another door that is ajar. After he finishes his business and pulls up his pants, he nudges the door further and takes a peek into the adjacent room.

Well, well, whispers the man with the crooked nose to himself.

On every wall, from floor to ceiling, are vintage bottles of wine, vodka, rum and champagne. Sonoma. Napa. Naples. Venice. Tuscany. Avignon. Marseilles. Madrid. Lisbon. Leningrad. Bottles of sake too, the Japanese lettering on its label indecipherable.

But what catches his eye more than the bottles on the wall is the one bottle that is already open and sitting by a used and empty glass at the far end of a long table at the center of the room. He walks up to the bottle and pours it into the empty glass. He sniffs the red wine and takes a gulp, strong and sweet. He quickly guzzles down one glassful, then starts another.

The cellar, eh? He can get used to this. He sits at the head of the table, alone and at ease for the first time that night, numbing his head to the point of almost forgetting about the loaded pistol inside his overcoat or the buck-toothed orphan boy who has promised to deliver the very person he aims to kill.

GRACE.

Gracie.

Grace.

Gracie.

Grace.

Gracie.

SOMETHING HITS his shoulder and jostles him awake. It is the brown boy with the buckteeth, shaking and naked save for his underwear, a welt swelling purple below his eye.

How long had he been sleeping?

The boy can barely get the words out.

The mayor, he says. He's in one of them moods of his again. I thought he was gunna kill me. I just couldn't go through with it. He said he was gunna pay me for it, but I couldn't bring myself to do it.

Do what? says the man with the crooked nose. His head has that familiar ache. It must have been hours that he was passed out at the table.

Grace.

Gracie.

Grace.

Gracie.

They are both dead, but the swishing of their names inside his brain has not let itself go.

I gotta get outta here now, says the boy. Before he sends his men for me.

Where is he? Where's the mayor? The man with the crooked nose pulls out the pistol from inside his overcoat. Startled yet half-grinning with excitement, the boy reels backward into one of the table chairs.

I said where is he, boy?

He's upstairs.

How do I get upstairs?

Ya see that door over there? Go through there and follow it around—you'll see an elevator. Take it to the top. He'll be the third door on your left.

Alright. Ya gunna be okay, boy. That mayor—whatever he did to ya he ain't gunna do to ya ever again, that I can tell ya.

The man with the crooked nose takes his top hat from the table and puts it back in its proper place. The brown orphan boy stands frozen, staring at the strange man in front of him, his buckteeth chattering in the dim light.

Somethin the matter, boy?

Um. It's your head, sir.

What's wrong with my head?

Well, how come ya have shit on top of it?

187

I gotta run, boy. Wish me luck.
Good luck, sir.
Good luck, boy.

Mare.

    Mayor.

        Mare.

            Mayor.

        Mare.

    MAYOR.

By the time the elevator reaches the top floor, the man with the crooked nose forgets whether the bucktoothed boy had said left or right, but with only one of the two doors ajar, he leaves it to instinct that the ajar one is the one he wants, and tiptoes down the long and dark hallway, his horseshoed soles clopping against the hardwood floor, bracing himself to be jumped by one of the men in dark suits at any moment.

He makes it to the door. Should he nudge it open or should he kick it open?

He opens the door swiftly but carefully, and sees the mayor's glowing white head in the corner of the room, his eyes half-closed, his mouth half-open. His giant body sits upright in a child-sized bed, his gigantic hands on top of the comforter, his enormous teats exposed and sagging downward on his chest.

The mayor opens his eyes wider. So gray and serene, they are.

His enormous mouth begins to move: I knew you was coming. I didn't have to see ya for myself—I could just tell from the stench of ya on the way in. The boy with the teeth—he told me about how much ya stank. You been drinkin, son? Your hand is shakin.

I can shoot him dead right now, the man with the crooked nose thinks to himself, but I rather he get a good look at his avenger first.

Yessir. I helped myself to an open bottle in your cellar.

Ya mean the one that was on the table there?

Yessir.

Well. Guess it's true when they say we all drink from the same well at one time or other. Had me some of that very same bottle just before—couldn't finish it. Found it too sweet for my taste. How about you, son—ya like it?

Can't remember.

Can't remember? You must be one drunk son of a bitch if you can't remember somethin like that. Well. That bottle you were drinkin—it's more than a century old. I'd say ya gotta be an old soul to appreciate something that old.

Well. I am that, Mister Mayor.

Bet you are. Come closer, son.

I think I like where I am, thank you.

Suit yourself.

The mayor gargles something deep in his throat, then hocks it out into the darkness. So. That boy with the teeth—can't remember his name now— he said you was an orphan like the rest of them down there. Said you was small like a boy—I can see he was right about that.

I ain't no boy, said the man with the crooked nose.

You ain't no big man neither. Not if you gunna kill me with that gun of yours.

Well, you ain't no big man yourself, Mister Mayor. Not if you're into having your way with them little orphan boys you ain't.

Really? Is that so? Tell me, son. Them boys who've never been loved— what's wrong with givin those boys the love they desire?

I can think of a lot of things wrong with it, Mister Mayor. The man with the crooked nose has the pistol pointed right at the mayor's head, but the giant man maintains his serenity.

A lot of things, eh? You got a boy in your life, son?

I reckon I might've at one time, but if I did, he died before he was ever born.

Well. Sorry to hear that.

The mayor keeps his eyes on the eyes of the gunman but not the gun itself. It is as if he can see right through into the intruder's soul.

Ya married?

I had a woman. She's dead now too. And so is my horse.

Your horse? You had yourself a horse? Well, that sure explains the stench of ya. A horse-lover, are ya now, son?

I ain't your son.

Aw, come on now. Every man in this great city is my son—you are all my children. Every man, woman and child, no matter how old or what color.

I ain't from the city.

You ain't?

I ain't.

Well. Then perhaps you ain't one of my children then. But tell me, mister horse-lover, now that you've lost your child, your woman, and your horse too, whom do you turn to give your love to now?

No one. I love no one.

Not even yourself, eh?

Nope. Not particularly.

Well. Can't say I'm not with you on that one.

The mayor's great white chest heaves forward and back at a slow and steady pace. The man with the crooked nose imagines it catching the bullet like a glove, squeezing the lead out between the breasts.

So tell me, says the mayor. If you ain't from the city, what's your beef then with me? Sounds like your beef should be with God, not me. Why me, son?

It was your decree.

My what?

You heard me, Mister Mayor. I said it was your decree.

Decree? I have a decree? What decree?

The man with the crooked nose clears his throat, his voice booming from the shadows: By executive order, it shall be, after ninety days, unlawful to operate a horse-drawn vehicle or offer transportation to the public on a vehicle drawn or pulled by horse. Any violator of said ordinance will be subject to criminal prosecution to the fullest extent of city law.

The mayor grins a devil's grin at the gunman's recital, his eyelashes aflutter.

So. You were one of them horsebuggers now, were ya?

That's right, I was. A horse-and-buggy driver. Yessir.

And you stand there with your pistol pointed at my head thinkin you're a better man than me? A man who made his livin treatin horses like slaves, breaking every bone in their body, in their mind, in their spirit, so you can earn yourself a few bucks and pretend to support the family you never had? That makes you a better man than me?

You shut your goddamn mouth.

You stand there with your forty-four aimed at my head and blame me for causing all your pain and sufferin when it was you who chose to make his livin as a goddamn no-good stinkin horsebugger?

Ya better stop using that word, Mister Mayor.

Horsebugger. Yeah, that's what you are, alright. A goddamn horsebugger. Gettin your rocks off watching them horses jiggle them buttocks at ya all day.

You shut your filthy face right now.

Tell me, son. Ever think about fuckin one of them horses? Ever think about doing that? Or were ya too short to get yourself up in there?

I had me no problems at all, Mr. Mayor. Had me a stool made just for the occasion.

Well, well. There you are. Child of the devil. That's what you are, son. Child of the devil.

Guess we're all the devil's children. At least some of the time.

Guess we are, son. Guess we are.

The gunman with the crooked nose had aimed for the mayor's gigantic head before he flinched his own eyes and pulled the trigger, but somehow the bullet he shoots from his old man's forty-four ends up in the giant man's lap, the blood turning the comforter to red all in front of him.

The mayor bellows in agony, lifting the comforter off his lap, revealing the frail naked body of a brown boy, face down over his crotch, the back of the boy's head rupturing in an afterbirth of red and purple brain matter.

My son, wails the white giant. You've killed my son.

In the dark of a child's bedroom, two grown men weep. One man cries out for the slain child, having finally accepted him as his own. The other man cries out for the understanding that, while he himself is indeed a killer, he had not the cold-blooded heart of one.

The teary-eyed gunman hears the sounds of footsteps in the hallway and the shouts of men rising up through the floors of the mansion. He draws the drapes in front of him and opens the only window in the room. Peering down from the window, he sees that it would be a steep drop but perhaps not a fatal one. As he shoves the forty-four back into his coat, he climbs onto the windowsill and contemplates just how in god's name did that bullet land where it had landed.

Who knows?

God knows.

Just another one of life's cruel miracles, says a voice inside his head. Why must it be the children who suffer the most from the conflicts of men?

Leaping from the window ledge, he imagines watching himself from below, a man attempting to land on his feet after a lifetime of repeated failure to do just that.

Woe, Grace. Woe.

TAKE ME to the first train station outta the city, says the man with the crooked nose, wincing in pain. He had limped a good two avenues or so before finding an empty cab.

The cab driver pays no heed to his instruction, his attention focused on the voice over the radio.

I said take me to the first train station outta the city.

What's that, chief?

Are ya deaf? I said take me to the first train station outta the city.

Oh. Okay then. First station. You got it, chief. Sorry bout that. Was busy listenin to the news. Did ya hear?

The man with the crooked nose feels his ankle swelling under one of his boots, his shin throbbing in the other. They feel more like sprains to him than broken bones, but the pain is excruciating nonetheless.

No, I didn't hear nothin.

It's the mayor's son. You know—that kid with the big afro? Someone killed him. Right inside the mayor's mansion. Shot him right in the head. Bang.

That so?

Yup. That's what they're sayin anyways.

Amazin how fast news travels these days.

Like lightnin, right? Bet ya when Lincoln was shot most people didn't know for a day—maybe even a week.

Never thought of that before. But I suppose you're right about that.

Yeah. Well. When you do what I do for a livin, it makes you think a lot, ya know? Same thing with my old job.

What old job was that?

I was one of them fellas who drove them horse-and-buggies you used to see around the city here.

The man with the crooked nose sinks a bit in the backseat, as much from the pain as from averting being recognized. He reaches for the top hat on top of his head—the very one he wore for driving horse carriages—to hide his face, but then remembers how it must be somewhere out on the mayor's front lawn, if not in police custody by now.

Ever taken a ride on one of them buggies? asks the cab driver.

The man with the crooked nose tries to sneak a peek at the driver's face, but all he can see are his brown eyes sticking out from under his cap in the rearview mirror. He looks at the cab license photo on the back of the driver's seat, but does not recognize the man with the long, shoulder-length hair staring back at him.

Nope. Can't say that I have.

Well, I don't know if you know this, but the mayor—he banned them here in the city. About a year or so ago. Just banned it just like that. Lost my job. Lost me some really good health insurance too. So what they did to us was they gave us a free cabbie license. We didn't have to train for it or nothin—they just gave it to us. First I was like, hey, don't tell me what I should do for a livin now and why should I work for the city that basically fired me in the first place, but, ya know, it's tough out there finding a job—ya know what I'm sayin?

Hear ya loud and clear. Been there—believe me.

Yeah. Well. So I ended up takin it—this here cab job, I mean. They were gunna make me into one of them station operators at first, but I was like fuck that, man—I wanna be out here on the streets, so I can think, ya know? It's important for a man to have some room to think, don't ya think?

Yessir. Nothin like having room for your thoughts.

Ya know, ya kind of look familiar.

The passenger's fingers dig into his trousers.

Really?

Yeah. Or maybe you just have one of them faces people always think is familiar to them—I don't know. But I tell ya somethin. I know this sounds real bad, but I wish whoever shot that poor kid in the head had shot the mayor instead.

Really now? Whoa.

I know. Ya think I'm bad for thinkin that, don't ya now?

Nah. Not really. I mean—no, not at all. Given what you've been through with losing your job and all, I can understand where you're coming from.

Ya can?

Sure. We all have feelins like that sometimes.

Like I said, I just think a lot, ya know? Maybe too much sometimes.

Yeah. Me too.

Hey. Do ya mind if I roll my winda down? Kind of smells funny in here.

Sure. Go on ahead. Guess I've gotten used to it now.

What's that? Got the wind blowin in my ear up here.

Never mind. Just ramblin my mouth off.

Yeah. Well. There's a lot of that going around.

Yep. There sure is.

ON MONDAY, the tiny black bug eats through two dead birds. But the bug is still hungry.

IN THE PREDAWN hours of a Monday morning, a lone man with limping legs and a crooked nose disembarks from the train that brings him to the town he has called home his whole life. Through the window of the station house, he sees the old station vendor behind the concession counter, snoozing upright on his sitting stool.

Oh, how I envy his idle life now, thinks the man with the crooked nose to himself. Its quietude, its consistency, its predictability.

The injured man limps his way through the town's main square, its shops still closed, its surrounding houses still dark, the sound of the plaza fountain the only sound that can be heard.

As he winds his way down through the woods on the dusty road and comes within sight of his farmhouse, his limp, while showing no signs of improvement, no longer seems to pain him as much as numb him.

When he reaches the row of hickory trees and steps onto the gravel driveway, he sees that his house has had a visitor, perhaps several, their brown footprints on the front porch steps. His eyes follow their trail and when he raises his gaze, he sees the consequences of their unexpected visit: the front door as well as the windows—high and low, from one side to the other—are all boarded up by planks of wood, layer over layer over layer, not a single square inch left uncovered.

He always knew this would happen. It is the very reason why he always came home every night. Just one night away from his home—that was all that it took for his nightmare to come true.

For a moment he worries that perhaps what happened in the city the previous night and what has happened to his home are interrelated and shudders at the thought, but he is soon able to convince himself, rightly, that the two events are unrelated—at least in any tangible manner. For is it not a wicked irony when a man with a home to call his own decides to crash a festival for feeding the homeless, only to limp his way back home to find that his home is a home that is no longer his own to live in?

He grabs the railing on the porch steps and helps himself down. As he limps toward the barn, he sees the sign that has haunted his dreams for so long, its big red letters: FORECLOSURE, and then: FOR SALE.

It is wicked, yessir. Wicked indeed.

The barn is boarded up too, its big doors bolted in. He thinks of his horse, his Gracie, and wonders had she been in there when the banking men had arrived what they would have done with her.

Let her go? No sir.

Shot her in the head? Probably not.

Have her put to sleep? Most likely.

Had their way with her? In his nightmares, yessir.

The man turns to face the pasture in front of him, its grass taller, limper and deader than ever, when he hears a low growl coming from around the far side of the barn.

Twinks. Is that really you? I thought you was a ghost or somethin. Guess you're all I got now. Thanks for waitin.

The growl of the brown and white dog gets louder as it ambles a step or two closer.

Easy now, Twinks. Everything okay? Easy, boy.

The man with the crooked nose crouches down gingerly to pet his companion, but as he reaches out his hand, the dog bites down hard, between forefinger and thumb, shaking its head back and forth over and over like a mutt gone mad.

The man with the crooked nose yelps in pain and swats the dog on top of the head with a hard slap, but the crazed canine clamps its foamy mouth down deeper and deeper, its eyes yellow and infected.

A few more painful cries and a few more swats later, the dog releases its jaws from the man's hand, leaving the flesh mangled and violet as it scurries away back around the barn.

What the fuck, Twinks?

A good dog until the last bite, yessir.

Hand and legs wounded, the man rolls over on his back in front of the barn. In the sky, he sees the sun beginning to rise, its blood-orange circle rising above the hickories.

Oh, Grace. Let me sleep forever.

But even a man with a crooked nose can smell trouble around the corner. It would be just a matter of time before the sounds of sirens would fill the air and men with dogs much more vicious than his canine companion would be combing the grounds.

He lifts himself up off the ground and looks out over the pasture again, toward the hills, where the woods lie beyond.

The woods. To the woods he must go.

But for how long should he stay there in those woods?

Until my wounds have healed some, he figures. At least the ones that are flesh and bone anyways.

He begins the long limp over the tall grass, the sheaths and spikes rising over his small body, his hands pushing him through like a blind man in the thickest of labyrinths.

Somewhere along the way, he hears the buzzing sound from above, as a family of flies converts his brown head into their new mobile home.

ON TUESDAY, the tiny black bug eats through three dead squirrels. But the bug is still hungry.

IT IS NOT until he reaches the woods that his head starts to throb and the fever sets in. He looks left, he looks right, he looks up, he looks down, but every object around him—the trees, the bushes, the fallen branches, the squirrels and chipmunks scampering about—takes on a hazy form of itself, as if everything is made of liquid and fog. He scratches the inside of his ears as they begin to itch and ooze and sees the blood on his fingertips, his bitten hand more black now than purple in color, with a gooey white moistness festering above the wound.

Rabies? Is this the rabies? The man with the crooked nose considers this, but quickly casts it away from his fevered thoughts.

You're thirsty. You must find water.

He drags and shuffles his tired feet over weeds and fallen leaves, his feet tripping now and then on an unseen tree root, causing him to stumble—to the ground, at times—but he manages to get himself up from every fall and march on.

A piercing pain reverberates up his legs, but he knows it is not related to the previous night's injury but to whatever has begun to ail him this morning since he entered the woods.

He whispers to himself as he walks. It ain't the rabies, no sir. Can't be that. Can it just be nerves then? Can't be that neither. How can my ears be bleedin from just nerves? And my throat—that hot buildup in there? That ain't nerves, no sir.

Feeling the congestion up his nose, he stops to pick at his nostrils. Dark red and green droplets string across his fingers like aged Christmas tinsel.

What in god's name is this? he wonders, but somewhere deep inside his mind he knows there is something familiar about all this.

He hops over a boulder, and when he gets to the other side of it, a pain sharp and excruciating shoots up into his chest, sending his body to the ground in a convulsive jerk. On his back, looking up through the hovering branches above, he wonders if this is the moment it all ends.

He shuts his burning eyes and then reopens them, the world above him melting all around him. He rubs his eyes at the corners and looks at his hands.

More blood. More mucus. More pus.

Grace.

He whispers her name, knowing whatever had gotten inside her body had now gotten inside his own.

Oh, Grace. The pain you must've suffered.

The branches above him begin to fizz. Birds become liquid comets. The flies buzzing around his face twinkle like stars.

He shuts his eyes and waits for the drone to end, but instead falls into a short nap. When he awakens, everything he sees is clearer than ever. The pain and weight on his chest has fully subsided. His nose, ears and eyes no longer ooze. Even his hand and legs feel like they were never wounded. Fully reinvigorated and then some, he starts to search for water again. He is still thirsty, but not as intensely as before.

Grace, he says aloud. You've come to save me.

He says it again: Grace. You've come to save me.

He stops to hold his ears, then says her name aloud again.

Grace.

He says her name aloud once more, only this time he shouts it at the top of his lungs.

Grace.

It is then that this poor soul with the crooked nose realizes that he is as deaf as he is lost. He screams up at the trees, and watches a blackbird take flight.

On every branch sits a banker. In every banker's bloodstained hand is a gray, or a brown, or a blue, or a red briefcase.

The bankers look down at the man with the crooked nose.

The man with the crooked nose looks up at the bankers—he does not know what to do.

Finally, he speaks to them: You bankers, you, he says, shaking a shit-stained finger at them. You must give me back my house.

But the bankers only shake their bloodstained fingers back at him and say, Tsz, tsz, tsz.

ON WEDNESDAY, the tiny black bug eats through four dead rabbits, then belches a tiny bug belch.

But the bug is still hungry.

THE BROOK is shallow, but deep enough for him to cup its water with his hands. He cups the water again and again for several minutes, then slides his body up against a small boulder by the bank. While his vision is still clear, it is not as acute as it was earlier. His ears still deaf, he is a tired and weary man again, his energy no longer elevated.

Something makes the water ripple in front of him. He follows the trajectory across the brook and finds himself face-to-face with the same category of beast that had attacked his beloved mare so many months ago.

He remembers the pistol in his overcoat, but knows it will take too long to fire. Besides, given the previous night's events, who knows where the bullet would land?

He would be better off trying to shoot himself instead—an idea that had been lingering in his mind for some time now, but perhaps was now too late to act upon.

Alright, ya furry devil. Ya gunna come over here and gobble me up for shootin your friend's foot off, are ya? Well, then hurry up and do it then.

The furry beast lowers its head and seems to ponder the invitation for a moment, then turns around and quickly trots off.

Where was it going? the man wondered. Where the food is, yessir.

The water intake having rejuvenated his appetite, the man with the crooked nose gets up from the boulder, walks across the brook, and tries to find out where the wolf has wandered, an endeavor pursued by only the maddest of madmen.

As he follows the subtle tracks in the dirt made by the beast, the sound of his own feet crunching over the fallen leaves gets louder and louder in his ears, his hearing gradually starting to come back to him.

The track of pawprints slowly begin to disappear as the layer of fallen leaves begins to thicken over the dirt floor of the forest. No longer on the wolf's trail, the man with the crooked nose decides to give up on his mad and futile pursuit and head back toward the brook, but as he turns, his eyes lock on a cluster of very large boulders, arranged by nature in a way as to form a cave with an opening only wide enough and high enough to allow only the smallest and shortest of men to gain entry.

Well, the man with the crooked nose says aloud. They won't be foreclosin on me here anytime soon. The return of the sound of his own voice nearly brings him to tears.

He is halfway into the cool and damp confines of the cave when he sees animal excrement on the floor, dry and rock-like, but this observation does not alarm the man for the cave had the air of abandonment the moment he stepped foot in it.

It takes an abandoned soul to know one, yessir.

Going as far back inside his new shelter as the outdoor light would allow him, the man with the crooked nose drops to the floor of the cave and sits there still for a moment, hearing the echo of the air and of his own breath. Looking at the wound on his hand, he can still see it, and feel it, festering, creeping its way up his lower arm like a small insect. He dips his finger in the red of it, then holds his finger out against the wall of the cave, ready to trace out the name that echoes eternal inside his mind, no matter what state it finds itself in.

Just as he finishes smearing the letter G on the cave's wall with the infected fluids of his injured hand, a cold and tingly sensation swallows him whole, embracing him down into the deepest of all slumbers.

ON THURSDAY, the tiny black bug eats through five dead raccoons, coughing up their whiskers.

But the bug is still hungry.

THE SWARM ASSEMBLES once again, braving the first gales of the incoming winter, buzzing with grief and anguish for its hallowed leader.

The Great White Giant stands at the pulpit of his city's most esteemed church, along with his wife, her brownness a shade paler, her elegance as woeful as ever, her attire all black from her shoes on up to her veil. At the foot of the pulpit, their son's serene figure lies on its back, facing up toward the celestial architecture of the church's ceiling, in a casket opened to the mural angels above.

The giant man's whispery utterances, somber yet soothing, echo throughout the chamber, his eulogy for his son mending the broken heart and nourishing the wounded soul of each and every fly-by mourner, as they sit in pews and bow their heads with a pensive drone.

And for the broken man who committed the heinous crime and remains at large, he offers four words: I forgive you, son.

As the swarm disperses to disseminate the latest message over each and every news web—Mayor Forgives Killer as City Mourns—the Great White Giant waves farewell in solemn appreciation for the grieving congregation, steps down from the pulpit, and leads the long procession up the center aisle, his dark-suited flock in tow, shaking hands with family and friends, officials and associates past and present. Somewhere behind him, the singing voices of children—a choir of castaways—overtakes the din of the great chamber, their funeral hymn reverberating from stained glass window to stained glass window.

The king of love my shepherd is, whose goodness faileth never.

When he reaches the vestibule, the Great White Giant embraces a small boy, as bucktoothed as he is brown, assuring the youngster that, while his heart might be forever broken, his love for the city's children will not be buried with his son.

I nothing lack if I am his and he is mine forever.

On Friday, the tiny black bug eats through six dead skunks, slurping up the foul spray from their tails.

But the bug is still hungry.

Me and my boy—we was out huntin in them woods over yonder a few months back. Told him I'd let him shoot the rifle this time. My son—he's about yea high. Small fella. But a big mouth, yessir.

Anyways. We got to talking about deer and I was tellin him about the first one I shot when I was a boy—it was a doe, ya see—and when I got to describing it, he says to me, Hold on there, Daddy. Ya mean to tell me that not all them deer have antlers?

I looked at the boy like he was a goddamn idiot. I was thinkin who grows up around these woods here not knowin that some deer have antlers and some don't? Less we're talking about reindeer, but we don't have any of those in these parts, no sir. I mean, I was about ready to call up that school of his and give them an earful, but my boy—he's such a darlin little fella—I just got myself down on one knee in the snow and told him about stags and does. You shoulda seen his sweet, little face when I told him—it was like his whole world opened up. He says to me, I guess I never seen a doe before, Daddy, and I says to him, Well, I guess you haven't then. He then asked me if there were any does in these here woods and I says to him, Where there's stags, there's does. And he said, How come we never seen any then, and that's when I told him to shut it, that if he kept up his yappin he'll scare away every goddamn doe and stag in these here woods.

He shut it mighty quick then, yessir.

So, me and the boy—we was walking for quite a bit not seeing nothing except for a rabbit here or there when we suddenly heard this shufflin sound coming from the ground up ahead of us. We could hear the sound of sticks being broken, bushes being shaken, so I knew, whatever it was, it had to be somethin big. Crouching myself down a bit, I pointed my finger to where the sound was coming from and whispered that he should stay behind me but stay close.

My boy, he sure yaps a lot, but he listens real good too.

So, I pushed on ahead, followin the shufflin sound, the sound of it gettin louder and louder as I walked, and when I reached the clearing, there was this brook, ya see, and up ahead there was this creature-like thing, down on all fours, its face in the water so I couldn't see it real good. It seemed to have fur on some parts of its back and on its side, but where there wasn't any fur, you could see that there were these blisters everywhere, only they were much larger than any blisters I've ever seen. More like craters, really. They seemed to be festerin a mighty bit, but the creature—it didn't seem to pay it any mind, no sir. It seemed very weary, and even sickly perhaps, but as painful as it all looked, this creature thing didn't seem to be bothered none.

So, it's just sittin there, the creature, very calm on the edge of the brook with its face in the water, when I decide to go ahead and tiptoe in a bit closer to have me a better look—it was still a good twenty yards or so away, ya see—and about five yards in, I can see it startin to lift its head up. I can see some fur on its face, but I still can't tell what in the hell it is since its face was still facing sideways on me, ya see. So, I get my rifle aimed and ready just in case, and just when I'm about to pull the trigger, this creature—it pulls its face out of the water there, and looks over my way.

Man, I tell ya. My skin might as well crawled right off my bones right then and there when I realized the creature was not some deer or other animal, but a man. He had welts and blister spots all over his face, and his nose looked all slanted like it could slip right off of him. But his eyes—that's what I remember the most. They looked they were bleedin on the inside, all red where the white should be, his eyeballs kind of yella-like. And that fur he had on him—it looked like it wasn't his, but from some other animal—like a fox or a wolf maybe—and it looked like it was stickin to his skin by some sorta feces or somethin. I'm not sure if the feces were his own or from some other animal, but since I was no more than ten yards away from the son of a bitch, I can tell ya he stunk to high heaven, yessir. Never smelled somethin so god awful in my life.

But this man-creature, it just stayed right there where it was, all calm-lookin, just waitin for me to make my next move. My boy—I must admit, I was so focused on what was in front of me that I had almost forgotten all about him. But my boy, he taps me on the shoulder and whispers to me, Well, Daddy—are ya gunna shoot that there doe there or what?

Yep. Doe. That was what he said.

Like I said—not the brightest bulb, my boy.

Of course, I told him no. Told him to back away. I lowered my rifle and just left the fella on his furry hands and knees. I looked over my shoulder just once to see if it was followin us, but the man-creature, it was gone. I remember thinkin maybe it was Bigfoot or somethin, but the man-creature—it was just too short and small to be anything like that.

So, me and my boy—we went on home and didn't talk about it. He once asked about it later, and I told him it was just a very sick doe. He being so gullible and all, he believed me, of course.

But me and my boy—we waited another couple of months or so before going out into those woods again. I let him shoot the rifle the next time, and ya know what? He shot himself his first stag, antlers and all.

Here—see my boy in this photo right here? That's him standin right next to its head on the wall right there.

A cute little critter, he is, ain't he? My boy, I mean? Sure is a darlin sweet fella, yessir.

On Saturday, the tiny black bug eats through a dead snake, a dead fox, a dead wolf, a dead deer, a dead bear, a dead horse, and one dead baby, and then drowns in its own bug vomit.

But the bug is still hungry.

So it bites its own leg off.

HOLD STILL, God. Hold still, goddamn You.
   Good Boy.

Hello? Grace? Will ya marry me, Grace? Will ya marry me?
Neigh twice if you'll marry me.

Gracie GRACE Gracie GRACE Gracie GRACE Gracie

GRACE Gracie GRACE Gracie GRACE Gracie GRACE Gracie GRACE

Gracie GRACE Gracie GRACE Gracie GRACE Gracie GRACE Gracie

GRACE Gracie GRACE Gracie   GRACE Gracie GRACE Gracie

GRACE Gracie GRACE

Gracie GRACE Gracie

GRACE Gracie GRACE

Gracie GRACE Gracie

GRACE Gracie GRACE

Gracie GRACE Gracie

GRACE Gracie GRACE

Gracie GRACE Gracie   GRACE Gracie GRACE Gracie GRACE Gracie

GRACE Gracie GRACE   Gracie GRACE Gracie GRACE

Gracie GRACE Gracie   GRACE Gracie GRACE Gracie

GRACE Gracie GRACE Gracie GRACE Gracie GRACE Gracie GRACE

Gracie GRACE Gracie GRACE Gracie GRACE Gracie GRACE Gracie

GRACE Gracie GRACE Gracie GRACE Gracie GRACE

The author of this book would like to thank his publisher, Jacob Smullyan, for his belief and blessing; Royce M. Becker for her artistry and vision; and his wife, Jennifer Sidel, and their two sons, Zachary and Samuel, for their love and affection. He would also like to thank Esphyr Slobodkina and Eric Carle for those times when inspiration presented itself.

Photo by Jennifer Sidel

JOSHUA KORNREICH is the author of three novels: *The Boy Who Killed Caterpillars* (Marick Press, 2007; Dzanc Books, 2013); *Knotty, Knotty, Knotty* (Black Mountain Press, 2014); and *Horsebuggy* (Sagging Meniscus, 2019). His work has been featured in various publications, including *Unsaid, Heavy Feather Review, Radioactive Moat, Meridian, Trop* and *Necessary Fiction*. He lives in New York City with his wife and two sons.

Printed and bound by PG in the USA

FICTION

After a nefarious yet revered mayor bans horse-drawn carriages in his city, reclusive horse-and-buggy driver loses his job, his lover, and his unborn ch[ild] as the desolate farm he has lived on his whole life deteriorates around him al[ong] with his sanity. But this lone wolf vows revenge. With language lean and lyri[c] and humor dark and grotesque, *Horsebuggy* is not only a haunting portrait [of] what happens when man's capacity for intimacy and acceptance is undermin[ed] by his more violent and sadistic impulses, but also a tragic love story an[d] penetrating study of how we destroy ourselves as much with our moralism a[nd] self-righteousness as with our vice and self-indulgence.

· · · · · · · · · · · · · · · ·

"Herein lies the tale of the crooked-nosed man—driver of a horse-dra[wn] carriage, and Grace—his rain-soaked, bedraggled fare. Kornreich delivers us the joy that comes to the lonely when love is found, and the anguish t[hat] ensues when love succumbs to suffering and, finally, to loss. And yet, for [the] crooked-nosed man, physical desire lives on, his unbridled lust to be satis[fied] only by the surviving object of his love, as reason unravels and he teeters tow[ard] lunacy. Told with stunning candor, Kornreich brings us an unforgettable tal[e of] tragedy, exploring the depths of both compassion and depravity. Get ready [for] the wildest of rides."
—Pamela Ryder, author of *Paradise Field*

"*Horsebuggy* roars along with comic verve, mythic gusto, and a tender, ta[rt] take on equine affections. Joshua Kornreich's exacting and entrancing pr[ose] rhythms provide momentum and delight. Climb up and take the ride."
—Sam Lipsyte, author of *The Ask*

"This is what *Citizen Kane* would have been if instead of a newspaper magn[ate,] it would have given us a character not unlike Lester Ballard from Cor[mac] McCarthy's *Child of God*, and if Rosebud had been an aging horse instead [of] a sled. A funny, transgressive, and oddly humane novel in which each fin[ely] wrought sentence leads you into a place of more desperation."
—Brian Evenson, author of *A Collapse of Horses*

Sagging
Meniscus
SaggingMeniscus.com

ISBN 9781944697747
90000

Cover design by Royce M. Becker